Henry Roe

A Review of the "Address of the Lay Association to the Laity of the Diocese of Quebec"

SALZWASSER
VERLAG

Henry Roe

A Review of the "Address of the Lay Association to the Laity of the Diocese of Quebec"

Reprint of the original, first published in 1859.

1st Edition 2022 | ISBN: 978-3-37512-792-3

Verlag (Publisher): Salzwasser Verlag GmbH, Zeilweg 44, 60439 Frankfurt, Deutschland
Vertretungsberechtigt (Authorized to represent): E. Roepke, Zeilweg 44, 60439 Frankfurt, Deutschland
Druck (Print): Books on Demand GmbH, In de Tarpen 42, 22848 Norderstedt, Deutschland

A REVIEW

OF THE

"ADDRESS OF THE LAY ASSOCIATION

TO THE

Laity of the Diocese of Quebec."

~~~~~~~~~~

IN A LETTER

FROM A

CHURCHMAN IN TOWN

TO A

CHURCHMAN IN THE COUNTRY.

———————

QUEBEC:

PETER SINCLAIR, JOHN STREET.

1859.

A REVIEW

OF THE

"ADDRESS OF THE LAY ASSOCIATION

TO THE

𝕷𝖆𝖎𝖙𝖞 𝖔𝖋 𝖙𝖍𝖊 𝕯𝖎𝖔𝖈𝖊𝖘𝖊 𝖔𝖋 𝕼𝖚𝖊𝖇𝖊𝖈."

———

IN A

LETTER FROM A CHURCHMAN IN TOWN TO A CHURCHMAN IN THE COUNTRY.

———

"If any man seem to be contentious, we have no such custom, neither the Churches of God."—1 Cor., xi., 16.

"Let nothing be done without the Bishop, in matters pertaining to the Church."—S. Ignatius' Epistle to the Church of Smyrna, cap. viii.

Ignatius was ordained Bishop of Antioch, within *thirty-six* years of our Lord's death, *by the Apostles themselves.*

As Alexander Borgia was wont to say of the expedition of the French to Naples that they came with chalk in their hands to mark up their lodgings, and not with weapons to fight; so I like better that entry of truth which cometh peaceably, with chalk to mark up those minds which are capable to lodge and harbour it, than that which cometh with pugnacity and contention.—*Lord Bacon*, Advancement of Learning, Book II.

QUEBEC:

PETER SINCLAIR, JOHN STREET.

1859.

"High time I think it is to give over the obstinate defence of this most miserable, forsaken cause (*i.e.*, the cause of the Puritans against Bishops); in the favor whereof neither God, nor, amongst so many wise and virtuous men as antiquity hath brought forth, any one can be found to have hitherto directly spoken. Irksome confusion must of necessity be the end whereunto all such vain and ungrounded confidence doth bring, as hath nothing to bear it out, but only an excessive measure of bold and peremptory words, holpen by the start of a little time before they came to be examined. In the writings of the ancient Fathers, there is not anything with more serious asseveration inculcated, than that it is God which maketh Bishops; that their authority hath Divine allowance, that the Bishop is the Priest of God, that he is Judge in Christ's stead, *that according to God's own law the whole Christian fraternity standeth bound to obey him.* Of this there was not in the Christian world of old any doubt or controversy made; it was a thing universally everywhere agreed upon. What should move men to judge that now so unlawful and naught, which then was so reverently esteemed? Surely no other cause but this: men were in those times meek, lowly, tractable, willing to live in dutiful awe and subjection unto the pastors of their souls; now we imagine ourselves so able every man to teach and direct all others, that none of us can brook it to have superiors; and for a mask to hide our pride, we pretend falsely the law of Christ, as if we did seek the execution of His will, when in truth we labor for the mere satisfaction of our own, against His."—Hooker, Book vii., § 16, 9.

"If they [the Romanists] would bring unto us such a Hierarchy wherein the Bishops shall so rule, as that they refuse not to submit themselves to Christ; then, surely, I should account those men worthy of even the severest anethema who do not submit themselves reverently, and with all obedience to such a Hierarchy."—Calvin, Tract de Ref. Eccles. iv., 1.

A REVIEW

OF THE

"ADDRESS OF THE LAY ASSOCIATION

TO THE

LAITY OF THE DIOCESE OF QUEBEC."

We have now, I suppose, the whole Synodal controversy fairly before us. The "*Lay Association*" have issued their *Address*, which, as it has been three months in preparation, may be fairly regarded as the mature result of their united wisdom and knowledge. The controversy has now assumed a definite and distinct shape, and is very considerably narrowed in its range. The points on which there is difference among us, as to the constitution of the Synod, are reduced to *two*, or at the most *three*. We may be thankful for this, for now there is some hope that misconceptions will be removed, that no more time will be wasted over irrelevant points, and that our differences may be fairly, fully, and temperately discussed.

I trust, however, that we shall hear no more of the "uneasiness and alarm," felt on one side only, respecting what is now confessed to be the most important question at issue, and that *we* shall not be again upbraided, as we have been[*], with making

---

[*] See "Letters of Anglican," &c., *Quebec Gazette* Office, 1857, page 16.

this point "the cherished idol, in comparison with which all other topics fade away in the distance of comparative indifference." It was not those who defend the Bishop's rights that raised this question at the first. The rule that in a Diocesan Synod nothing should be done without the concurrence of the Bishop, was a principle universally recognized; never, in the whole history of the Church (except in one single instance, which, after all, is no fair exception), departed from. We looked on the rule as a matter of course. A number of persons baud themselves together to overthrow this principle, and because we rally in defence of it, they charge us with being the authors of the disturbance, and with making a minor matter to be the only point of any importance. Now the mask is dropped, and the " Lay Association" openly declare themselves to be united mainly for the purpose of preventing the recognition of this, as we hold it, essential principle in the constitution of the Church of Jesus Christ.

Now I wish to say, at the outset, my dear friend, that, for my part, I cannot object absolutely to such an Association as this, considered in itself. I cannot say, because I do not think, that it is an unlawful thing, under any conceivable circumstances, for a number of Christians, of whatever order, to unite together for the preservation of the rights and privileges of the Church of God, or for the restoration of some important privilege or right, of the exercise of which she had been deprived. But I do say that, on the very face of it, this *Association* bears evidence of a character which should make every loyal Christian pause and hesitate and think well before he joins it.

The Clergy, it is confessed, are the teachers and guides of Christian people, God's ambassadors, the ministers of Christ, and stewards of His mysteries.* An Association, then, which *sets itself* to excite distrust of their pastors in the minds of the people, to sow dissension between them, to persuade the

---

* Eph. iv. 11, 12; Heb. xiii. 7, 17; 2 Cor. v. 20; 1 Cor. iv. 1; St. Matthew, xxviii. 19, 20.

people that their pastors are seeking to usurp authority over them and to deprive them of their rights, is something which ought not to commend itself, at first sight, to the goodwill and confidence of Christian people. Whether this be not a fair account of the object of the " Lay Association," or at least of the means they take to attain their object, you may judge from the following extracts from their own pamphlet.

The Bishop, at the request of the Clergy, in the summer of 1857, appointed six laymen to act as a committee, with six clergymen, to draft a form of constitution for the Synod. This was done to save time, that a form of constitution might be ready to be submitted to the Synod for consideration at its first meeting, and that the Clergy and Lay delegates might not be at the expense and trouble of coming together to do nothing more than appoint a committee, and so go home again In this, say the *Lay Association* (Appendix, p. 2), the Clergy, "while yielding a semblance of respect for Lay rights, violated them;" and what they did on that occasion was "unprecedented, unconstitutional, and contrary to law." At the meeting of the 24th June, the conduct of the Clergy "resembled too closely *those unseemly contests for the maintenance of usurped authority* which stain the earlier pages of the history of the Church" (Appendix, p. 4); conduct which "aroused and justified feelings (on the part of the Laity) which have been since still further outraged." "The disorder," of that meeting, "was excited," as the *Lay Association* "believes," "by the *tone and bearing* of those (the Clergy) to whom the Church is wont to look for patterns of forbearance and decorum." (Appendix, p. 5.) The "policy" of the Bishop, &c., is stated to have been up to that time carefully concealed, "until the second resolution of the prepared series developed *the design* of transferring to a few lay delegates associated with the Clergy the functions which the law had confided only to the Church at large." (Appendix, p. 3.) The subsequent steps taken by the Bishop, which resulted in the Amending Act, are stigmatized (Appendix, p. 6) as "a specimen of ecclesiastical diplomacy, an example of the exercise of party zeal, but little calculated to foster the confidence of the people in their rulers, or to win for the persons of those who exercise administrative power in the Church the respect which their office should at least (*sic!*) deserve." The *Association* declares (Appendix, p. 6) that the Bishop's action on this occasion " it is impossible to forget and difficult to forgive." They describe the Amending Act (3rd Res., Appendix, p. 8) as an " insidious" plot against the rights of the Laity, and " well calculated to retard the prosperity of the Church, and perhaps permanently impair its best interests." (4th Res., Appendix, p. 8.) They declare that the Bill " revokes and curtails the powers of the Church" (Appendix, p. 13); that the Bishop's "interposition" was " uncalled for," and the "influence" which "prevailed" to carry the Bill was " sinister."

These extracts are all taken, it is true, from the *Report* in the *Appendix*. But that violent and unscrupulous "document," for which some excuse might otherwise, perhaps, have been charitably found, as a not unnatural outbreak of the disappointment and irritation of a party defeated in their (as they thought them) so well concerted schemes, is now, after three months of calm reflection, adopted and endorsed by the *Lay Association*.

The *Address* itself, however, though less violent in expression, is, in its spirit at least, as bitter as the *Report*. Its aim is plainly to make a breach between the Clergy and the Laity. I need but refer you to the insinuation (on the 8th page) that "the question" that lay delegates ought to be communicants, " is mooted *to exalt the sacramental power of the Clergy* " (whatever that means); and to the contemptuous manner in which the whole body of the Clergy are spoken of (p. 20) as the mere creatures of the Bishop, whose " votes" he can at any time " command."

I say, then, that on the very face of it this *Association* wears an aspect which ought to excite the alarm and arouse the suspicions of all sincere Christians. Love and peace and unity are the marks by which our Lord would have us to be distinguished—that we may all be one in Him, as He and the Father are One. The ministry was given for the very purpose of building up the Church into this unity and love. (Eph. iv. 11, 16.) Those must be very grave faults in the Ministers of Christ which can justify any man, or body of men, in systematically exciting against them, in the people to whom they minister, distrust, contempt and hatred.*

Here, then, is perhaps the proper place to enquire, are these serious charges against the Bishop and Clergy well founded? Have they been and are they still engaged in a conspiracy to deprive the Laity of their liberties and to usurp power to themselves? And are the members of the *Lay Association* in reality united together to defend the invaded rights and liberties of their brethren?

The very audacity, my friend, with which these groundless charges are alleged, makes it difficult to refute them. The simple truth is, that the opposite of all this is the fact. The Clergy have, all through this struggle, been contending for and maintaining the rights of the whole body of the Laity, which a party of disloyal Churchmen in the city were attempting to usurp, and finally to deprive them of.

The Laity have hitherto had no share in the general government of the Church in these Colonies, nor, indeed, have the Clergy. The object of the Synod is to give them both a share in that government, *an equal and co-ordinate share.* With whom did the Synod movement originate? Not with the *Lay Association*, but with the *Bishops*. And who pushed it on strenuously? Not the *Lay Association*, but the *Clergy*. Did the Laity ever seek this power for themselves? Did they ever complain of their exclusion? Did they ever heartily join in the movement, and warmly help it on? No, emphatically, no! This is power which they neither sought nor desired, but which has been literally thrust upon them. The Bishops and the Clergy have had to urge and press this matter upon their brethren year after year, until, through their exertions, seconded by a few zealous laymen, the end was accomplished. Does this look like a wish to usurp power over the Laity, and rob them of their rights?

---

* The London *Record*, in a late article against the attempt to revive the Confessional in England, says: "At any rate, let not any who love Protestant Truth, whether Clergy or Laity, be carried by over zeal into widening the breach between ministers and people. That is the result which Satan wishes to bring about."

8

Consider next the meeting of the 24th June, and the history of the two Acts of Parliament. To entrust "the framing of constitutions and making of regulations" for the Church to a mass meeting of the Church people of a diocese like this was a proposal rather too extravagant and too novel* to have been for a moment entertained, much less conceived, by our Legislature. The Bill was drawn up for, and adopted by, the Synod of Toronto, composed of Bishop, Clergy, and *lay delegates*,† and was intended to remove all doubt as to the legality of what they were doing. Would they have tried to remove those doubts by making all their proceedings absolutely illegal? To suppose this involves an absurdity.

A flaw, however, was discovered in the *Act*. The *first* meeting, it was alleged, would not be legal if the Laity were there by representation. It must be a *mass meeting* of the Laity, but need only be a *pro formâ* meeting, to comply with the letter of the *Act*. No hint was breathed, till the day came, that it was to be considered a meeting empowered to draw up a Constitution for the Synod. The Bishop suffered himself to be prevailed upon. He issued his circular calling such a meeting for certain specified purposes. These were, *first*, to adopt the Act; and *secondly*, to provide for the representation of the Laity in all future meetings of the Synod. Notice was given accordingly, by reading this circular, or the substance of it, in every church and chapel in the Diocese, as well as by advertisement in the newspapers of Quebec. The resolutions‡ prepared by the Committee of Clergymen and Laymen who had drawn up the form of constitution, and proposed at the meeting, *simply embodied the circular;* and yet it is said that "no announcement or disclosure was made of the intended policy"!

---

* English Legislatures and Englishmen love *precedents.* Perhaps some learned member of the *Association* will furnish us with a few precedents. or even *one single example* in the history of the Christian Church, of *the whole Laity of a Diocese* coming together to legislate for the Church.

† See "Proceedings of the Synod of Toronto in 1856," pp. 17, 18, 19.

‡ The proposed resolutions were those which had a short time before been adopted by the first meeting of the Synod of the Diocese of *Huron*. See the Bishop of Quebec's "Letter," of the 31st August, 1858, p. 6.

Till that moment, certainly, the party who have since formed themselves into the *Lay Association* had "afforded no notice" of *their* "proposed proceedings." Though everything "had been (to use their own language, which most exactly describes their own line of action) prepared in private for the occasion, —there had been no announcement or disclosure of their contemplated policy, until" Mr. Jeffrey Hale's amendment "developed the design of transferring" to *themselves* the most important function of the Synod, a function upon the right discharge of which, according to their own shewing, "EVERYTHING *depends*" (p. 23), that of drawing up and adopting a Constitution. Their plans had c inly been admirably laid. under the guidance of some master mind. All, from the highest to the lowest, had been well drilled in the parts they were severally to act,—some to argue lucidly and learnedly, and some to shout lustily and to abuse vociferously. A Committee to be ballotted for had been selected, and their names,* —most of them extreme party men,—printed on ballotting tickets, and distributed secretly among the adherents of the party in the meeting. That Committee was to draft the Constitution, and report to an adjourned mass meeting in Quebec, by which it was to be adopted, and so *finally and unalterably fixed*.

Every man with the least reflection must have seen, by a glance at that meeting, that a large majority of any adjourned meeting in Quebec would be composed of the blind and excited adherents of that party. The Clergy saw this. They clearly perceived that if they consented to what was proposed, they would be betraying the rights of their flocks, and that the liberties and privileges of the Laity of the whole Church would be gone for ever ;—they would, at best, be but helping to

---

* Here are the names, that the Church may judge whether she could entrust with confidence to them the drawing up of her Constitution : Six Clergymen—The Lord Bishop (a mere clergyman, and to have no more voice in the drawing up and adopting of the Constitution than any clergyman or layman) ; Rev. Dr. Percy, Rev. Dr. Hellmuth, Rev. Mr. Sewell, Rev. Mr. Thompson of Stanstead, Rev. Mr. Reid. Six Laymen—Mr. Jeffrey Hale, Lieut.-Col. Fitzgerald, Mr. Christian Wurtele, Mr. Andrew Stuart, Mr. Buchanan, Mr. Scott.

work a Synod whose Constitution was drawn up and adopted and unalterably fixed by a few laymen of Quebec.

I am not exaggerating the importance of this matter of drawing up and adopting the Constitution of the Synod at first. It is the estimate of the *Lay Association* themselves. "EVERYTHING," say they (page 23) *"connected with the well-being and efficiency of the Church,* whose Protestant doctrines, discipline and formularies are the inheritance which ought to be handed down to posterity unimpaired, *will depend,* under Providence, upon the character which she, as now called upon, may give to herself as an institution Synodically organized with all the authority of law. EVERYTHING WILL DEPEND *upon the nature and provisions of the* CONSTITUTION, which it will be the first duty of the Synod to construct." These, then, were the interests at stake on that occasion,—these, and nothing less, the powers this party in Quebec made so open and determined an effort to transfer from the united deliberations and equal votes of the Bishop, the Clergy, and the deputies of the whole Laity of the Diocese, to themselves. The Clergy, therefore, not so much in defence of their own rights (for if they had yielded, besides all the popularity they would have gained, they would have been permitted to choose the six clerical members of the Committee, and also have had secured to them the right of voting as a separate order), as for the sake of their Lay brethren, who were there neither in person nor by representation, firmly, and for the moment successfully, opposed this bold and open act of usurpation. And the Laity of this Diocese owe their Clergy a lasting debt of gratitude, which will yet, I am satisfied, be acknowledged and paid. It is for this successful stand against a party, who counted on no such obstacle to their ambitious projects, that the Clergy have been assailed with so much virulence, and "their conduct and bearing" on this occasion,—conduct and bearing which, under the circumstances of the case, when truly represented and fairly considered, reflect on them the highest credit,—grossly and cruelly misrepresented.*

---

* I cannot avoid calling special attention to the second foot-note on page 20. A statement is there repeated which was first (I believe) made

There is evidently but one way in which the whole Laity of a Diocese like this can meet in Synod, and that is by representatives. The Diocese extends from Stanstead, 150 miles above Quebec, to Gaspé, 500 miles below it. The means of access to the place of meeting, select it where you will, are, from most of our missions, tedious, and from all expensive. The mass of our Laity, as well as our Clergy, are poor. They are, on the lowest computation, 25,000 in number. To say to the whole church-people of such a Diocese as this, "you must *all* come together," is practically to disfranchise the greatest part of the Diocese, and to give over the powers of the Synod into the hands of those few who live in and near the place of meeting. It was evident, after the meeting of the 24th June, that this was the only way in which the Act, thus interpreted, could work. The Legislature saw this at once, and, notwithstanding all the influence* which was brought to bear upon them, common sense prevailed ; and an *Act* was passed, unanimously in the Upper House, and by a vote of *seventy-two* to *seven* in the Lower, *every Churchman in the House voting for it,* which *secures to the Laity* of the whole Diocese those rights of which the members of the *Lay Association* so strenuously and perseveringly sought to deprive them.

Now, my dear friend, who, in the name of everything that is reasonable, were most sincerely concerned to vindicate the rights of the Laity ? Was it the *Lay Association*, who, under the shallow pretence of giving to every single Churchman in the Diocese an actual share in the framing of the Constitution, sought to shut out the Laity in all other parts of the Diocese, and to keep the whole power in this matter, on which " everything connected with the well-being and efficiency of the

by Mr. Jeffrey Hale, in a speech at Quebec last summer, and shortly after publicly contradicted in a letter to the *Quebec Mercury* by the clergyman in question,—the learned and eloquent Dr. Falloon, of Melbourne. This statement, coming as it does after Dr. F's. own public explanation, must be considered as intentionally insulting and injurious to Dr. Falloon,—not personally, but as *one of the Clergy*, with a view to set them all wrong with their flocks.

* And the praises of the *Lay Association*. See Resolution 1, and Petition; Appendix, pp. 9, 10. I cannot help thinking that this 1st Resolution was intended to be (what it certainly would be if the Legislature *merited* the praise) *most severely sarcastic.*

Church will depend," in their own hands? Or was it not rather the Bishop and Clergy, who, amidst such a storm of abuse and misrepresentation as they have been assailed with, contended for and secured, not to themselves, but to *all the Church-people in the Diocese*, an *equal share* in the making of laws for the Church and managing her affairs?

Putting apart, then, all other considerations, and simply looking at these facts, is this an Association worthy of the confidence of the Laity? They take great pains to impress on our minds (Address, p. 4, and Appendix, p. 14) that "the Laity of the city have no inducement to over-reach the Laity of the country." This is a very different tone towards the Laity in the country to that assumed at the meeting of the 2nd of Sept., when they hoped to prevent the passing of the Bill. Then they tried to fill the Laity of the city with jealousy and fear of their brethren in the country.* They complained that in the amending Act "the principle of representation by population had been scouted, *and the Laity of the City almost ignored;* that "under the amended law, *Quebec would always be in a minority.* They say they "have no inducement to over-reach the Laity of the country." Why, then, did they try to do so? No, my friend, it is not the rights of the Laity they are concerned to secure. These are men, the leaders among them at least, to some of whom certain peculiar views in religion are dearer than life, and these they will have adopted, at all costs and hazards; others of them seek the gratification of their own private or family piques; and others again the aggrandizement of their own personal consequence. No! they have now exposed themselves completely, and if the Laity of the Diocese put confidence in them now, all I can say is, "Populus vult decipi, et decipiatur."

II.

I have detained you long over this first point, but it is one of much practical moment. I come now to the consideration of the two (or three) important points on which the *Lay Association* differs from the views and practice of the Church at large.

---

* See their own full account of this meeting, in the *Quebec Gazette* of September 6th, and the report of the speeches then made.

1. The first is "the qualifications of the Lay delegates." The *Lay Association* object to the rule that Lay delegates should be communicants. The reasoning of the *Lay Association* under this head, if not convincing, is at least novel. After describing this rule as "a needless and dangerous interference with the elective franchise of the people," (p. 7), they go on to say: "The idea has nevertheless *more than once been seriously proposed*, to limit eligibility to the office of a delegate to communicants." This is, certainly, an extraordinary way of speaking of a qualification which is the rule in *every Diocesan Synod* in the British Colonies ;* which, moreover, is the rule in several *of the Diocesan Conventions* of the American Church†, and is being gradually, year after year, adopted by them all; and which was adopted, in 1856, *as the rule of the* GENERAL CONVENTION *of the whole American Church !* It certainly is *true* that "it has been more than once *seriously proposed* to limit the office of delegates to communicants," but is it *the whole truth ?*

The *Lay Association* tells us (p. 7) what "the *motive for the proposal* may be *presumed* to be." The motive which urges and must always prevail with Christians to establish this rule, is surely very simple, and such as a plain man can easily understand. It is this: that a Christian, who is living in the open breach of his Saviour's dying command, and in the wilful neglect of the highest means of grace, cannot be fit to legislate for the well-being of that Saviour's Church.

But the *Lay Association* proceed to say : "It is difficult to discover why, out of the *whole catalogue* of the doctrines,

---

* That is, in Huron, Toronto, Nova Scotia, Adelaide, Melbourne, Cape Town, New Zealand, Christ Church, and Tasmania.

† It is the absolute rule in Ohio, Virginia, (the two most noted "Low Church" Dioceses in the American Church,) and Vermont. It is "recommended to the Churches" of South Carolina ; and a Canon, unanimously adopted, of the Diocese of New York, declares that "the welfare and prosperity of the Church require, and it is in itself proper and right, that no Lay delegate should be sent to this Convention but such as are communicants of the Church." There may be other instances ;—these are those in which I have ascertained the rule to exist. See Hoffman, p. 191.

moral requirements, *sacramental* and ceremonial observances of the Church, one in particular should be selected as the only stepping stone to Synodical honours." This passage, my dear friend, is so extraordinary, and I may add instructive, that I must ask you to pause over it for a few moments. Ordinary men only attain a clear knowledge of the more recondite principles of things after they are already found out to their hand, by long and painful study and laborious thought; it requires creative genius to strike off so brilliant a discovery as this with a cursory flourish of the pen. These great facts, however, we must in justice allow, are not so uncommon among distinguished eclesiastical agitators of our age and country. The Hon. Col. Vereker astonished the religious world three or four years ago, and even took Exeter Hall by surprise, by publicly declaring and maintaining manfully that the Church of England *held but one Sacrament.* It remained for the *Lay Association* of Quebec to discover in her system "*a whole catalogue* of *sacramental* observances"!

May I be permitted, with great deference and submission, to suggest to the gentlemen of the *Lay Association*, whether the reason "why, out of *the whole catalogue of sacramental observances*," the Holy Eucharist is selected as the qualification "for so important a trust," may not perhaps be this : That, as all "members of the Church of England" are *baptized* in their infancy, the *only Sacrament remaining* in which Lay delegates *can* partake is the Holy Eucharist!

But, seriously, my dear friend, are the *Lay Association* in earnest, or are they gravely jesting with us, in writing in this slashing, haphazard sort of way? What does it mean?

"Difficult to discover why, out of the whole catalogue of doctrines, moral requirements, sacramental and ceremonial observances, the Holy Eucharist should be selected as the test of eligibility" for Lay delegates! This is mere nonsense. The Holy Eucharist is not a doctrine, neither is it a moral requirement, nor yet a ceremonial observance. It never was in "the catalogue" of these things, and cannot, therefore, be "*selected out*" of it. It is one of the two great Sacraments which Christ has ordained in His Church. And one purpose for which it is instituted, and has always been used among Christians, is "to be a badge and token of Christian men's profession," "to put a visible difference between those who belong unto the Church, and the rest of the world."

And yet the *Lay Association* tells us "it is difficult to discover why it should be selected" for this purpose! It may be difficult for the *Lay Association* to *discover* this,—for their powers of *discovery* are, we must acknowledge, not to be measured by ordinary rules; but to plain, sensible people, I apprehend there will appear no such difficulty.

The *Association* speak of the Eucharist as being made "the stepping-stone to Synodical honours." This irreverence is worthy of grave rebuke. Synodical honours are a very small matter in the eyes of the Church. Obedience to the laws of Christ, and common consistency before men, are things much more important.

They assert that it is made "the sole test of eligibility to this important office," as if to require this excluded all consideration of other tests of fitness. This would be just as much as to say that, *because* all candidates for parliamentary honours must take the oath of allegiance, *therefore* the different constituencies are precluded from choosing fit and proper persons, and are obliged to take *any one* who should choose to take the oath of allegiance! The cases are precisely similar. The Church at large has a right to demand the guarantee that all who are to join in making her laws and carrying on her government *shall be full members of her communion.*

It is not desired to limit the choice of particular parishes or cures, any further than to require that none shall be sent to the Church's Synod who are not in *full* membership with her. Within these limits the choice is uncontrolled. And, with a sincere regard to piety, what other course than this can the Church pursue?

The *Lay Association* speak of this rule as an act of "partial legislation in the wide and delicate question of personal Church discipline." But this is plainly a misapprehension. The whole question of Church discipline turns, not upon the point whether members of the Church shall be required to be communicants—*that* point Jesus Christ himself decided for all ages when He said, *Do this*,—but upon this, viz : the conditions upon which persons shall be admitted to, or the offences for which they shall be excluded from, the Holy Table. To say that none shall be Lay delegates but communicants, is not to enter on any delicate question of Church discipline; it is simply *to take the discipline of the Church as it is.* It does not interfere with the terms, right or wrong, on which members are admitted to the Communion ; but requires that from those thus pledged as full members of the Church the persons must be chosen who are to share in the solemn deliberations of the Synod.

I do not deny that if " the godly and wholesome discipline of the Church were restored, which were much to be desired," (though this, in my humble opinion, is much too large and grave a question for any single Diocesan Synod to entertain,) there would be a better guarantee of the fitness of communicants for this office ; but what we say is, that under *our* circumstances, it is the *best*, and, under any circumstances, the *only* guarantee the Church at large can have of the soundness in faith and practice of her members.

Yes, this is the reason why it is and ought to be selected ; because it is *the sacrament*,* and, as such, the constantly renewed oath of allegiance to Christ and His Church, emphatically "the badge and token of Christian men's profession ;" (Article XXV.) and, above " all the catalogue of doctrines, moral requirements and ceremonial observances," it is selected because it *includes* them all, requiring, as the qualification for receiving it, "repentance towards God and faith towards our Lord Jesus Christ," and binding the recipient by the most awful of all sanctions,—the Body and Blood of Christ,—to universal holiness of heart and life, and thus being itself, as Bishop Jeremy Taylor says, " an *epitome* of the Christian Religion."

---

* Or *oath*, as the Latin *sacramentum* means. So Pliny, a pagan Governor, giving an account of the Christians to the Emperor Trajan says : " They bound themselves (in their assemblies) by an *oath* [sacramento] not to commit any wickedness." " To take the sacrament upon a thing " is a phrase among the common people to this day.

Even in these days of lax discipline, the approach to the Holy Communion is guarded in some degree against the unworthy. No man can be a communicant, if the pastor does his duty, who is guilty of any open and scandalous sin, besides that such men are not very likely to offer themselves. No one but a grossly dishonest man can join in the communion service of our Church, if he is unsound in the faith. And it is to be presumed that no man would do so, with so many other respectable religious bodies around him, to any one of which he can, without reproach, join himself, unless he were intelligently and loyally attached to her system. It is, therefore, the best pledge the Church can have of the moral purity, the doctrinal soundness, and the loyal attachment of her members. And though this *best* pledge may be, after all, no *absolute warranty* of fitness, yet since it is the most *probable*, we are bound to use it; according to the celebrated dictum of that profound Christian philosopher Bishop Butler: " Probability is the guide of life." May not this possibly be a reason why it is "selected"?

But there is another consideration, which may perhaps render it less "difficult" for the *Lay Association* "to discover" why Lay delegates ought to be communicants. The Church of England herself has spoken with authority on this subject, and has established this as the *test*, not only of fitness for all the offices to which she admits the Laity, but even of adult membership itself. She requires *all parishioners* (8th. Rubric, at end of Holy Communion Service) to communicate *at least three times a year*. And I need scarcely remind you that the Church's severest punishment, as the very word *excommunication* shows, is to cut off offending members from the Lord's Table. How, then, can those who wilfully excommunicate themselves be fit to fulfil the solemn office of legislators in the Church of Christ? How should the Church deem it right to entrust the power and privilege of legislating for the whole body to non-communicants, when she has judged (Canon XXIX. of 1603,) that none but a communicant is to be entrusted with the nurture of even a Christian infant?

But this test of membership is not confined to the Church of

B

England. Among all the Protestant denominations (except the Quakers, who reject both the Sacraments altogether,) there is not one which recognizes any persons as *members of the Church*, or as *having a right to vote on any Church question* except the *communicants*. Hence, I remember, that when last year the Diocesan Convention of Massachusetts voted against the necessity of this qualification in its delegates, they were twitted by a dissenting newspaper with having decreed, that "personal piety was not required in a legislator of the Episcopal Church!"

The *Lay Association* bids us "remember, that conscientious scruples of various kinds deter some *consistent* members of the Church from approaching the sacramental table," and that a man "may be a moral and *conscientious* Churchman," and yet not a communicant. In answer to this it is sufficient simply to deny that such men are either *conscientious* or *consistent* members of a Church which peremptorily requires, as an elementary principle, all her members to be *communicants*.

But they urge further, "May not this very *tenderness of conscience* which actuates them [*i.e.*, to refuse to come to the Lord's Supper] itself supply the strongest possible security, if accepting the functions of a delegate, that they will faithfully and conscientiously discharge them?" Now, my dear friend, I confess to you that whenever I hear men of a certain party speaking of *tenderness of conscience*, I always instinctively put myself upon my guard. Dr. South's well known rule at once recurs to me, "When you hear a Puritan speaking of *conscience*, rest assured that he has a design upon your *pocket*, and that the word *conscience* is used only as an instrument to pick it." "What a rattle and noise (says he) has this word *conscience* made! How many battles has it fought! How many Churches has it robbed, ruined, and reformed to ashes! How many laws has it trampled upon, dispensed with, and addressed against! And, in a word, how many governments has it overturned! Such is the mischievous force of a plausible word, applied to a detestable thing."

And what sort of a conscience that was which he here calls a destestable thing he explains in another passage, where he says, "I cannot find (among the gifts of the Spirit) the gift of accounting *tenderness of conscience against law* as a thing sacred, and *tenderness of conscience according to law* as a crime to be prosecuted almost to death." Yes, my dear friend, this is just the old Puritan plea of a *tender conscience;* that very *tenderness of conscience* which once "laid in the dust the purest and most primitively reformed Church in the world," and is ready to do it again. It is not that true tenderness of conscience, which makes it quick and exact to spy out what is wrong in yourself, and to reform; to discern what is your duty and to fulfil it; but by it they mean a weak, ignorant, and ill-informed conscience, which is slow to see that a disagreeable duty ought to be done, and even when it does see this in some measure, always finds insurmountable obstacles in the way of discharging it. No, my friend, "this tenderness of conscience," which blinds a man to his duty of obeying his Saviour's command, while it puffs him up with spiritual pride, as if he were therefor a better man than his neighbour, is certainly no qualification in the eyes of any sensible man for any office of trust or importance. It is rather too much to ask us to believe that it "supplies the *best possible security* for a faithful and conscientious discharge of duty."

I do not deny that there are some good men, worthy to be communicants, and really prizing that holy privilege, who yet are kept back by "conscientious scruples;" but those scruples simply amount to this,—that they, in their mistaken and misleading humility, judge themselves morally unfit for so heavenly a feast. These, however, are men who would, with equal humility, shrink back from so great a work as that of legislating for the Church of Christ—they are the very men who would heartily and zealously support the rule in question, and resist any infraction of it. It is better, in any case, that the Church should be deprived of the wisdom and experience of many such men as these, than the last fragment which is left of her holy discipline should be thus contemptuously dashed to the ground, and the most positive law of her Divine Head trampled under foot.

But the *Lay Association* urges again that the "adoption of

the sacramental qualification for Lay delegates would, in this country, in some cases so circumscribe the choice of the people as virtually to destroy it," and that it would be an "*inconvenient*" enactment! The rule, I daresay, may work inconveniently for the purposes of the *Lay Association*, but, for the former argument, it is a libel upon the Church,—it is contrary to all experience to doubt that the most *devout* and *intelligent* of her Laity are and always will be communicants; for obedience to God is the truest piety, and piety is the truest wisdom.

To compare this rule—a rule universally established as I may say, in the Church of God, in this and every age—to the "odious and demoralizing Test and Corporation Acts," is worthy of the fairness and scrupulous honesty in the use of arguments which so strongly characterize the pamphlet of the *Lay Association*. The Test and Corporation Acts disqualified all but communicants of the Established Church for Parliament and all other public offices of trust and emolument in the kingdom. They thus held out a strong temptation to ambitious men among Roman Catholics and Dissenters (as well as among ungodly persons in the Church herself, among infidels, &c.) to be guilty of the profanity of receiving the Holy Communion in the Church, in violation of their conscience. We may readily grant these Acts to have been odious and demoralizing. But how is the rule requiring Lay delegates to be communicants a revival of the Test and Corporation Acts? It is scarcely supposable that worldly and bad men would become regular communicants merely to attain the poor honor of being Lay delegates. But if we can suppose such a case, there still remains this dilemma: that those worldly and bad men who had influence enough to get themselves elected, after openly profaning the Sacrament to gratify their ambition, would much more readily obtain their election if there were no test at all. If this test would not exclude them, then the absence of all tests would certainly admit them.

It is an unalterable law of the kingdom of Jesus Christ, that every member of His Church should be a constant communicant. And because some unworthy persons are found among those communicants, this cannot make it any the less our sacred duty to require that all who are entrusted with the high and holy work of legislating for and otherwise governing that Church should not be living in open violation of the most sacred of her laws.

We are told (foot-note, p. 9) that in two instances in the American Church, in the Dioceses of New York and Pennsylvania, efforts to introduce the rule requiring delegates to be communicants were "made and negatived." But the *Lay Association* forget to tell us that the same page of Hoffman (p. 191-2) from which they quote two of the paragraphs in that foot-note, supplies the information that, in the Diocese of New York, "a proposition to that effect" was *adopted* in 1848, though not confirmed in 1849; and,—what is even of more importance, as shewing the sense of that great Diocese upon the *principle* at issue,—that one of the *Canons* of that Diocese, adopted in 1802, is this: "That in the opinion of this Convention the welfare and prosperity of the Church require, and it is in itself proper and right, that no Lay delegates should be sent to this Convention but such as are communicants of the Church, and have been so for at least one year previous to their appointment; and that it is recommended to the parishes to adopt this principle." They do not mention that it would almost to a certainty have been carried in 1858, if the Bishop had not interposed his judgment, to which those excellent Churchmen at once deferred. They quote for us a part of what the Bishop of New York said on that occasion, when he was speaking of a case which in no way resembles ours; but would it not have been more to the purpose to inform us what that eminent man, on the same occasion, said *ought* to be done, if their case were what ours is? Here are his words: "The desirableness in the abstract of having the body of Lay delegates composed of communicants would, I suppose, be admitted by all. Indeed I believe things are tending to that result in this Diocese, as fast as circumstances will at all permit." It is only "the attempt to enforce it all at once, by a new rule, which changes the practice which has prevailed in the Diocese from the first," which he deprecates.

What do the *Lay Association* mean by suppressing the facts of the case in this wholesale way?

This pamphlet is put forth by the *Lay Association* to help you churchmen in the country to " form your opinions and principles" (p. 23) on these important subjects. To this end they profess to supply you with reliable " information" (p. 4) on the various points they treat of, and they invite you (p. 22) to give them your " serious and prayerful reflection." Is it consistent with these professions to suppress every fact that makes against the views they advocate; to say that it had been " more than once seriously proposed to require delegates to be communicants," when in every Diocesan Synod in our Colonies this is the established rule; to quote from a work a passage telling you of two cases in the American Church in which motions to adopt this rule were lost, and to omit the information which *the same page* of that work supplies, not only that Lay delegates must be communicants, in several Dioceses of that Church, but also that in one of the two Dioceses they quote, it has been, since 1802, the solemn and deliberate sense of the Convention that Lay delegates ought by right to be communicants ; and to make no reference to the all-important fact, that the *deliberate judgment of the* WHOLE *American Church* on this point was most emphatically declared, when, in 1853, it was adopted, and in 1856 by an overwhelming vote* confirmed, as an amendment to the Constitution of the General Convention, that all delegates must be communicants? What good end can this suppression of truth serve? Is this the best way to help you to form your opinions and principles on this subject?

You see, then, my friend, that in the *American,* as well as in the British Colonial Church, it has been something more than " *seriously proposed* to limit eligibility to the office of a delegate to communicants."

But were it otherwise, our case is not parallel to that of the American Church. American churchmen, in such cases as those quoted in the foot-note, page 9, are striving to throw out an old and long-established practice which the conscience

* See Journal of General Convention for 1856, pp. 64 & 67.

of the Church more and more disapproves of. We are about to lay down a right principle at the outset, in which we are following the "*prevailing* precedents" of the American Church as well as of every one of our own Diocesan Synods throughout the Empire. It is one thing to repeal a long-established, even though faulty custom, when by doing so peremptorily you would "cast out" of the Synod, and probably tempt to forsake the Church altogether, several exemplary members; but it is quite another thing to lay down a right principle at the beginning, which cannot possibly offend or drive away any. Let us be content with copying the excellences,—let us avoid the failings of the American Church, those errors which we see her now, though with pain and difficulty, gradually but firmly undoing.

III.

I pass by the third point considered in the *Address* (pp. 10, 11),—which I do not think of much importance,—merely begging you to notice how, in quoting from the " Minutes of a Conference of the British North American Bishops," the sentence, that the Bishops "considered it desirable that the Bishops, Clergy, and Laity in each Diocese should meet together in Synod at such times and in such manner as may be *agreed*," they quietly *drop out the Bishop,* and assume that the *agreement* spoken of is to be between the Clergy and Laity, the Bishop having no voice in the matter. This was scarcely what the Bishops meant, and it seems hardly fair to exclude them from any share in an *agreement* which they themselves were the first to propose, and which is to be on their part all surrender, and on ours all gain. It is quite true (and *note these words well*) that " the Synod once assembled will become the supreme authority in the Church in all matters affecting itself." (Address, p. 11.) But the *Association* ignores the fact that " the Synod " is composed of " the Bishop, the Clergy, and the Laity," and that nothing can become " a provision of the Constitution" which is not " consented to" by *each* of these three orders.

IV.

With the conclusion the *Lay Association* comes to as to their *fourth* point, the "vote by orders," I can have no quarrel; but I am sorry to have to complain of the same disingenuousness in stating the facts of the case here which I have already noticed more than once. They describe* (p. 11) the *vote by orders* (which I freely acknowledge they explain very lucidly) as a wholesome usage, conservative of the *rights of the Clergy* and Laity alike, obtaining universally in the Diocesan and General Conventions of the sister Church in the United States, and transcribed from her excellent models into recent organizations of the Colonial Church." This I suffer to pass; but when they go on to say : "It is utterly without precedent in the mother Church of England and Ireland," they must have known, and ought to have stated, that the reason why it is "without precedent in the mother Church" is, that the Laity have never yet been admitted to a seat or share in the Synods of the mother Church. How could the Laity and Clergy vote as two orders, where there were only Clergy and no Laity present ?

But if the mother Church of England furnishes no *precedents* for the vote by orders, she furnishes *analogies*, and those analogies all go to establish the principle involved in the vote by orders, as an inherent right, and not as a constitutional

---

* The "recent public document," by the way, which the *Lay Association* quotes (p. 11) one would scarcely conjecture to be *their own Report in the Appendix!* This is the same extravagant grandiloquence which transforms some obscure and anonymous Letter-writer in the *Quebec Gazette* in 1853 into "an English author" (p. 20), "an English writer" (p. 18), and, to cap the climax (p. 16), "a Church of England author of grave character and great experience"! One would naturally suppose, as I did at first, that this "Church of England author, of grave character and great experience," was the judicious Hooker, Sir James Stephen, Lord Brougham, or some other equally eminent English Jurist. Thus the only *authorities* these learned gentlemen can quote are themselves and some writer in the *Quebec Gazette*, under high-sounding and misleading titles, and the confessed and gradually relinquished defects of the American Church.

privilege. So far as English precedents go, Church Legislation, properly so called, is *confined* to the Clergy, in their Synods, and the Laity have no direct voice in the matter. But then, to balance this, Synods, Diocesan and Provincial, of the Church of England, are prohibited from making *Canons* without the consent of the Crown. Even with that consent such Canons do not bind the Laity without the ratification of Parliament, which was originally in reality, and is still in theory, the Laity of the Church by representation.* *Hooker* (viii. § 6, 8,) lays it down as a right, inherent in both Clergy and Laity, "that no ecclesiastical law be made in a Christian Commonwealth without consent as well of the Laity as of the Clergy. For of this thing *no man doubteth,* namely, that in all societies, companies and corporations, what severally each shall be bound unto, it must be with all their assents ratified. As the Laity should not hinder the Clergy's jurisdiction, so neither is it reason that the Laity's rights should be abridged by the Clergy."

V.

I have now reached the point which is confessedly the most important of all,—*the question as to the Bishop's right to a voice in the decisions of the Synod.* Here the *Lay Association* evidently have laid out all their strength to fortify the view they advocate. Besides passing reference to the subject all through the pamphlet, *ten* out of *twenty-two* pages (considering the foot-notes more than half of the Address) are devoted to this point. They have certainly put their arguments very cleverly,—as strongly and well, I suppose, as arguments on that side can be put. And knowing how much easier it is to argue *popularly* on their side of this weighty point than on the right side,—since they have prejudices and passions to appeal to, which we have not, and which we certainly should not try to arouse if we could,—I enter upon the discussion with much apprehension of not doing full justice to the subject,

---

* See Burns' Ecclesiastical Law, "Synods," and compare Hoffman on American Church Law, p. 184.

but at the same time with that confidence which a thorough persuasion of having the right always inspires.

The first thing that strikes me, after reading over carefully this part of their *Address*, is the absence of any fair and lucid explanation of the nature of the principle at issue, any clear statement of the question. This the Laity of the Diocese certainly had a right to expect from those assuming the task of giving them "information" on the subject. The *Association*, however, does not take this course. They give to the right, which we claim to be inherent in the office of Bishop, an odious name; and, without stopping to explain what that right really is, at once proceed to argue against it. Thus, a point which, if explained clearly and simply, would at once commend itself to every unprejudiced churchman of good common sense, becomes an awful phantom, looming mysteriously in the distance, big with terror, and charged with every element of tyranny and destruction. Here are the terms in which the *Association* speaks of it. It is "the Episcopal *Veto*" (p. 13),—"an absolute negative upon any measure of the Synod, carried by whatever separate majorities of both its orders,"—"an autocratic authority, such as that of the *Emperor of Russia*" (p. 20),—and "to hold it essential to the Episcopate is at once to *unconsecrate* upwards of thirty Prelates of the American Church." It is "a needless experiment,"—"an untried invention, at variance with the constitutional principles, prevailing precedents, and successful experience of the most perfectly organized Protestant Episcopal Church in the world." It "invests the Bishop with the power of *nullifying* the proceedings of the Synod,"—"entrusts" him "with *uncontrolled authority*." It is a "prerogative fraught with the greatest danger to the Bishop himself as well as to the Church." It is "the *one-man* power,"—"a power that would clothe its possessor with *an accumulation of prerogatives* not less *foreign* as a whole *to a scriptural* Episcopate, than would this one in particular be *dangerous to the independence of the Church*."

By this clever, but, I must think, rather dishonest expedient, the right claimed for our Bishops grows to be something terrible and dreadful beyond description,—a power, like that of the beast in Daniel, only for evil—suited, and but too likely to " devour and break in pieces, and to stamp the residue with his feet."

But what are the *facts* of the case? The Bishops are actually the autocratic and irresponsible governors of the Church. They have all the power they can desire. This power they are now seeking to share with the Clergy and Laity. They need not do so even now. The law does not compel them to call their Synods together; it permits them to retain things just as they are. For an irresponsible governor to call together a body of men subject to him, for the purpose of divesting himself of power and committing it to them, is at least not the most obvious way of seeking " autocratic authority" and uncontrolled power" !

And what share do the Bishops propose to give the Clergy and Laity in the administration of the affairs of the Church? *An equal and co-ordinate share with themselves.* They call in the aid of the Clergy and Laity, and agree that, without the consent of both, nothing shall be enacted, nothing carried into effect by the Synod. But in reality they give up a great deal more than this, because the body of the Clergy and Laity in a Synod must always have a vastly preponderating influence. Nearly every measure brought before the Synod will be originated, discussed, and passed by them ; while nothing can be enacted or done without them. This is to give the Bishop " uncontrolled power."

But this does not satisfy the *Lay Association.* The Bishop must, in the Synod, abandon all his prerogatives. It is not enough that he consents to do nothing without the Clergy and Laity, unless he further consents that they may decide and do anything and everything without him. Nay, more, he must now promise to *agree* to everything they enact, and even to carry it into effect, no matter how strongly he may be, in his judgment or conscience opposed to it.

This, however, is simply to abandon Episcopacy. And it is plain that if the Bishops do not retain the right of having a voice in the decisions of the Synod,—if they consent to give up their right of concurrence in what is done,—then, so far as the Synod is concerned and can effect it, *they cease to be Bishops and become mere Chairmen of Presbyterian Assemblies.*

It is not, my dear friend, it is not a question of increasing or diminishing the Bishop's power. The true issue is, *Bishops or no Bishops: shall we cease to be Episcopalians ?* For if in the Synod, the solemn council of the Church, when she is met in the name of God to consult and take action for the well-being of the whole body, you permit any and every measure to be carried without and against the Bishop's consent, then you take away from him, so far as the Synod's action extends, all his Episcopal functions. If the Presbyters and the people can carry any and every measure in the face of the Bishop's solemn refusal to concur in what is done, and then compel him as Bishop to carry into effect measures of which he disapproves, and bind him by Canons made by his own Clergy and Laity, to which he refuses his assent, then the Church is governed in reality, not by Bishops, but by Presbyters and Laymen. Henceforth we must define the word "Bishop" thus : "What is a Bishop? A Bishop is an officer of the Church, whose duty it is to see, under the direction of a Committee of Presbyters and Laymen, that the decisions of the Presbyters and Lay delegates in their Synods are carried into effect."

Let me remind you that this is nothing more than what is *distinctly claimed* by the *Lay Association* in their *Address.* They say (p. 11) and say truly, that "the Synod, once assembled, will *become the* SUPREME AUTHORITY *in the Church in all matters affecting itself.*" But "the Synod," according to them, is in reality the Clergy and Lay delegates,—the Bishop being merely the President of the Synod, and his concurrence being quite unnecessary to the passing of any and every measure. So that,—LET THE CHURCH PEOPLE OF THE DIOCESE MARK IT WELL,—what the *Lay Association* claim and wish to establish is this: that the Synod once assembled, the SUPREME AUTHORITY IN THE CHURCH, in all matters affecting the Synod, shall be, *not the Bishop, but the Presbyters and Lay delegates !*

Here I might stop and rest my argument. For if to give

up this point be so far an abandoning of Episcopacy, no more words are needed. The Anglican Church has contended too long, and suffered too much, in defence of the sacred rights of Bishops tamely to abandon them now. She knows what British Christians,—she knows what universal Christendom, in every period of its history, owes to Christian Bishops. To them the Christian faith was committed in the beginning to be kept and handed on, and to them, under God, it is owing that that Faith is now in the world in all its original purity. The government of the Church by Bishops, we believe, was ordained by her Divine Head, and established by His Apostles. *We are not prepared to give it up.*

But it is not the mere *name* of Bishops we desire. We want no shams in the Church of God; no empty, meaningless forms; no solemn mockery of investing our Bishops, at their consecration, with an authority which they ought not to possess, and which they are never to exercise. No! if we are to be churchmen, let us be so in reality. If our Church is to be governed by Bishops, let us leave them some function of government. They have given up all they can and all they ought. Let us imitate the noble example of the churchmen of Nova Scotia, and of Huron, and rally round our Bishops and call upon them to stand up for the Divine Constitution of the Church like men, and say to them, " Even if you *were* willing to betray the sacred rights committed to your trust, *we* dare not, cannot, will not permit it! We will still maintain unbroken that golden principle of unity which binds us to the Church of the Apostles and Martyrs, and binds the whole Church in one: LET NOTHING BE DONE WITHOUT THE BISHOP.''

This, then, my dear friend, is *the true issue* between the Church and the *Lay Association*. And when it is once made clear that it is so,—that it is not a question of giving more or less power to our Bishops, but of abandoning (so far as the Synod is concerned) or retaining Episcopacy,—I am sure that enough is said to satisfy any honest Churchman.

But to strengthen the case, let us proceed to examine the arguments of the *Lay Association* one by one. Their first point is the argument from authority; and this they dispose of with the greatest ease. In the American Church "there are upwards of thirty organized Dioceses in which the Bishops are clothed with no such prerogative," the small and unprogressive Diocese of Vermont (see Appendix A) being the solitary exception to the prevailing rule. "No other precedent (say they) has been produced, except that it has been very recently yielded, in *some* newly-formed Colonial Synods, with untried Constitutions."

Why does the *Association* adopt this extraordinary mode of speaking? Why say *some* Colonial Synods? Were they not aware that into the Constitution of *every one* of our Colonial Synods the principle is introduced that "no act of the Synod shall be valid without the concurrent assent of the Bishop, Clergy, and Lay delegates"? True these Synods are recent; the oldest of them only dating back to 1852. But then it must be remembered that these Synods were all professedly formed in imitation of the Diocesan Conventions of the American Church; and that, with the Constitutions of those thirty Dioceses before them, *every one* of our Colonial Synods, after the fullest consideration, deliberately dissented from them in this point. This fact is of great importance. The Anglican Church, in nearly every part of the British dominions*, has weighed, judged and condemned these American precedents. If we could consent (which God forbid!) to repudiate this principle, we should be opposing ourselves to the deliberate judgment and solemn enactments of the whole Anglican Church.

The precedent of the American Church, on which they so much rely, I will consider presently. But, meantime, *will they produce a single example, in the history of that Church, of a*

---

* That is in the Dioceses of Toronto, Huron, Montreal, (by vote at a meeting of Bishop, Clergy, and Lay delegates, 19th January, 1853,) Adelaide, Melbourne, Nova Scotia, Cape Town, New Zealand, Christ Church, (and in all other Diocesan Synods that may hereafter be formed in New Zealand), Tasmania, and Natal. The same principle is established in every Diocesan Synod of the Scottish Episcopal Church. See Hoffman p. 132.

Diocesan Synod, in which this right, when claimed by the Bishop, was deliberately repudiated? This, let it be remembered, and nothing less, would be a parallel to what they are proposing we should do in this Diocese.

The *Lay Association* says, "No other precedent," for the principle at issue, "has been produced," except those of Vermont and our "newly-formed Colonial Synods." If they mean precedents in the case of Synods formed in all points upon the same model as our own, it is true, but nothing to the purpose, because no other such Synods, besides those in the American Church, and in our own Colonies, have ever been held. The Laity were never admitted to deliberate and vote in any Synods of the Christian Church* until they were admitted by the American Church. But if they mean that there are no precedents in the case of Diocesan Synods, constituted as they were up to that time, they show themselves strangely ignorant of the controversy in which they assume the place of teachers.

Diocesan Synods,—composed of the Bishop and his Clergy, —have been held in every part of the Christian Church, from a very early age, and in the English Church in particular, constantly before, and several times since the Reformation. These Synods were required, by the Canons of the Church, to be held every year; and the principle on which they deliberated was this, that "nothing should be done without the consent of the Bishop." "Diocesan Synods," says Bishop Ken-

---

* See the amplest proof of this in *Suicer's* Thesaurus, s. v. Σύνοδος— where he describes *four* sorts of Councils held in ancient times, *all* composed of *Bishops.*

Jeremy Taylor on Episcopacy, sect. xli., headed "*Bishops only did vote in Councils, and neither Presbyters nor people.*

John Johnson's Clergyman's Vade Mecum, Vol. II., containing the Canons of the ancient Church, Pref. iii. 1, 2, who agrees with Taylor, and adds,—"That it is the particular privilege of English Priests, to have a right to sit as constituent members in Provincial Synods, and are owned in all conclusive Acts to have a negative on the Bishops."

Abp. Potter, Church Government, cap. v. of making Canons (p. 288, Philadel. Ed. 1824.)

net,* "have a better title to antiquity than Provincial Synods. The Bishop of each Diocese had an original right to convene his own Clergy, and, *with their advice and consent, to ordain* such rules and orders as were proper to declare the doctrine, and regulate the discipline of their own body." "The right existed in former ages," says Judge Hoffman, (p. 203) "of a full negative (by the Bishop) upon the act of any Diocesan Synod or Council." The sense of our Reformers on this question is to be seen in the *Reformatio Legum*, or Book of Reformed Ecclesiastical Laws, drawn up chiefly by Archbishop Cranmer. In this work provision was made for Diocesan Synods to be held every Lent; and there, among other things to our purpose, it is ordained in accordance with all former Canons of the Church, "That the decrees and sentences of the Bishop, published in his Synod, the inferior Clergy shall observe as valid."† In short the maxim of Ignatius, the martyred Bishop of Antioch, himself a disciple and friend of the apostles, "Let nothing be done without the Bishop in things pertaining to the Church," was a rule never departed from in the Catholic Church, until the rights and independence of Bishops, which are equally inconsistent with the papal supre-

---

* Kennet's Ecclesiastical Synods, Vol. ii, 109 and 180, as quoted in Hoffman, p. 181 and 132. The position of Bishop Kennet is abundantly sustained by the learned foot notes to pages 131 and 180, of Hoffman. See also, Bishop Gibson's *Codex*, under *Synods* and *Councils*.

† Quoted by Hoffman, p. 183, note. See also *Gibson's Codex* under "Councils" and "Synods." *Bishop Hall's* works, Vol. x; p. 434. *Dr. Thomas Jackson*, in the reign of James I., tells us that "he remembered with joy of heart the Synods of the Diocese in which he was bred." See his works. In Mason's life of Bishop Bedell, p. 209, we have a full length account of a Diocesan Synod held by him in Kilmore, in 1638, together with the Canons passed on the occasion. I need scarcely refer to the Diocesan Synod of Exeter, held in 1851, in calling which, the Bishop, whose opinion on the Law points connected with the Synod was confirmed, though unwillingly, by the Law Officers of the Crown, lays it down as a recognized rule (Pastoral Letter of 9th April, 1851, p, 113,) "that no resolution can be deemed an act of the Synod, which has not the Bishop's concurrence." See also the learned Bishop Hobart's judgement, quoted and confirmed by the Bishop of Toronto, in his address before the Synod of 1856. See "Proceedings of Synod," 1856, p. 12.

macy and the supremacy of distinguished but ambitious laymen, began to be encroached upon, and were finally denied and usurped by the Bishop of Rome. We may take up Bishop Jewell's and Hooker's form of challenge, and say to the *Lay Association, We require you to bring any one sufficient sentence out of Holy Scripture, or any Catholic Doctor, or Father, or Council, or any one example in the whole Christian Church, for a thousand years from the beginning, whereby it may plainly be proved that the Bishop, in his Synod, or out of his Synod, ought not to have the right, and we will yield up the cause.*

These, then, are our precedents for the principle that nothing should be enacted in a Diocesan Synod without the consent of the Bishop,—not the constitution of "Vermont, and of some recently formed Colonial Synod," alone, but *the Laws and practice of the whole Christian Church from the beginning, in every country of the world, and especially of our own Anglican Church, both in ancient and modern times;* while the single precedent that can be cited by our opponents is the omission of this rule in the Diocesan Constitutions of the American Church.

But, my dear friend, the case of the American Church is one of our strongest points; for, when fairly examined, it makes far more for us than, even when unfairly represented, it makes against us. Those who are so fond of bringing up this precedent on all occasions do not seem to have carefully studied the history of that Church. The subject is a large one, and most deeply interesting. To treat it fully would require a volume, but time and space permit only a very brief outline.

Look then, first, at *the circumstances of that Church at the time of its organization.* After being planted in those Colonies since the year 1696, the English branch of the Church still remained at the time of the Revolution without a single Bishop. Unceasing and zealous efforts had been made by the greatest and best men in the Church, to obtain the consent of the British Government to the appointment of Bishops, or even of one Bishop, for America. "Letters and memorials from the Colonies supply, *for a whole century,* a connected chain of such expostulations, yet still the mother country was deaf to their entreaties. At home they were re-echoed from many quarters.

C

34

Succeeding Archbishops pressed them upon successive administrations; and the Society for the Propagation of the Gospel, during almost every year, made some effort in the same cause. The records of those memorials show how earnestly and with what strength of argument it pressed this great cause upon the notice of the Government." (Wilberforce's American Church, p. 149.) The defeat of all these efforts was owing in part, it is true, to the remissness of Churchmen in the Colonies, but chiefly to the influence of the Puritans in America, and of the Puritan party at home, who held the balance of power in their hands, and whose threatened anger the minister of the day was ever afraid of provoking. Such was the state of feeling on this subject among the Puritans in America, that Bishop White says, "I have lived in days in which there existed such prejudice against the name, and still more against the office of a Bishop, that it was doubtful whether any person in that character would be tolerated in the community! * Thus within the Church there was no organization, no point of union, no power of increase. Schism tore the Church to pieces. Heresies unchecked desolated the flocks. One of the oldest and best endowed Churches in Boston openly apostatized to Unitarianism, and Socinian principles were avowed by some among the members of the Church, and suspected among many. One Lay delegate in the General Convention that revised the Prayer Book, proposed that the invocation of the Three Divine Persons, &c., of the Holy Trinity, at the opening of the Litany, should be omitted ; the Athanasian Creed was excluded altogether from the American Prayer Book, and it was not without difficulty that the Nicene Creed, which had been excluded from the proposed book, was finally preserved ; and the Revolutionary war seemed to have completed the ruin. The Church came out of that struggle with her temples burnt, sold, or destroyed, her property alienated, her ablest clergy, and many of her ablest sons, in voluntary or compulsory exile, and herself held in popular odium and suspicion, as not only monarchical in her organization, but also (her Clergy and

* Dedication to Memoirs of the P. E. Church.

people having, in general, been loyal in the war,) attached to Kingly Government, and as still looking with fond regret to wards that mother Country whose yoke the Colonies had just thrown off.

Besides this, many, perhaps the mass, of the Church people themselves, including many of the Clergy, who had never seen a Bishop, by listening to the increasing calumnies of the Puritans against them, had acquired an unconquerable fear of the tyranny of Bishops, and opposed their introduction. When, in 1771, the ninety-one Virginian Clergy were called together to petition the King in favour of an American Episcopate, after the second summons but *twelve* came, a majority of whom, after one opposite decision, agreed to the petition; but against this vote, two at first, and ultimately four, protested publicly; and such was the feeling of the Laity, that these four received the unanimous thanks of the lower branch of the Virginian Legislature "for their wise and well timed opposition to the pernicious project of introducing an American Bishop." Churchmen in North Carolina were for adopting a nominal Episcopacy, and "instructed their delegates to the General Convention of 1857, to insist, as a condition of union, that they should not be compelled to receive a Bishop." * The Legislature in Maryland entertained the plan, of themselves appointing ordainers; and even Bishop White, then a Presbyter, to whom, under God, more than any other man, is due the preservation of the American Church from utter extinction, shortly after the Revolution, despairing of Bishops being appointed, actually put forth a plan in print for carrying on the whole work of the Church without them ; proposing, among other things, to commit to the President of the Proposal Convention, and other Presbyters, the powers of ordination and discipline. † Of the danger which threatened the very existence of the Church at that critical period we may judge by what Bishop White wrote in his old age respecting the Convention,

* Hoffman, p. 154.

† Life of Bishop White, p. 80. Wilberforce's American Church, p. 191, &c.

which finally decided to seek the Episcopate from England—that "he looked, half with a remnant of uneasy sensation at the hazard which this question (of seeking the Episcopate) ran, and at the probability which then threatened that the determination might be contrary to what took place."*

The Legislation of a Church under such circumstances,—carried on under the jealous and suspicious eyes of a nation which scarcely tolerated them,—a Church without experience, without a shadow of organization or unity, with internal dissensions and weakness, with the plague spot of heresy breaking out upon her, with such low and destructive views of Episcopacy as were prevalent within her pale, and such bitter hatred of it without,—was not likely to be too favorable to the rights of Bishops. Instead of being surprised that some serious errors were made, we must, after a full consideration of the subject, ascribe it to God's special Providence that the Church in her integrity did not then perish from the land.†

Next, let me briefly trace out for you the rise and progress of the Legislation of the American Church, on the subject and the rights of Bishops.

In May, 1784,‡ the first influential meeting of Clergy and Laity was held in Philadelphia. One of the *principles* they adopted (the 5th) was this:—"That to make canons or laws (in the Episcopal Church in these States) there be *no other authority* than that of *a representative body of Clergy and Laity conjointly*." Here there is no mention made of Bishops.

In October of the same year, a more full and formal Convention was held in New York, when the above article was amended as follows:

"5th. That in every State where there shall be a Bishop

---

* McVicker's Life of Hobart, Vol. ii, p. 85. White's Memoirs, p. 132.

† For the matter of this section, see Hoffman pp. 87 & 110. McVicker's Life of Hobart, Vol. ii, cap. 4. Wilberforce's American Church, cap. iv & vii, and Bishop White's Memoirs of the P. E. Church, *passim*.

‡ This Synopsis is carefully abridged from Hoffman's work on American Church Laws, pp. 89, &c., compared with the "constitution, &c.," of the General Convention of 1856, and Wilberforce's eloquent History of the American Church.

duly consecrated and settled, he shall be considered a *member* of the Convention *ex officio*."

" 6th. That the Clergy and Laity, assembled in convention, shall deliberate in one body, but shall vote separately ; and the concurrence of both shall be necessary to give validity to every measure." Here Bishops are recognized and admitted as simple *members* of the Convention, but they are not allowed any privilege above any Lay delegate, not even that of presiding.

In June, 1786, the Convention known as "The second General Convention," adopted, as the 3rd article of the Constitution, that "Bishops might sit and vote with the Clerical and Lay deputies, *ex officio*, and that a Bishop, if any were present, *should always preside in the Convention*." This is a slight improvement.

In 1789 an amendment to this *Article* was adopted, to the effect that "when there should be *three* Bishops (and there were already *three*) they should form a separate House of Revision, and any act of the House of Deputies was to be sent to them for *concurrence;* but if they *refused* to concur in it, it should yet become law if *three-fifths* of the Lower House adhered to it." The establishment of a House of Bishops was a long step in advance, though their powers at the time were very shadowy ; for they were not allowed to *propose* any new measure ; and their solemn judgment, after being asked, might be set aside by a vote of three-fifths of the House of Deputies

In October, of the same year, this *Article* was further amended, so as to give the House of Bishops the right to *originate* acts ; and a vote of *four-fifths* of the Lower House was to be required to negative their decisions. And it was not till the year 1808, or *twenty-four years* after the first meeting of the Convention, that the right of the House of Bishops was fully recognized, and the article on this subject amended, to the effect, that no measure should pass without their concurrence. There still remained, till the last General Convention, a clause unworthy of the American Church, in this (the 3rd) article of her constitution. I mean, the provision that the House of Bishops must "signify their approbation or disapprobation (*the latter with their reasons, in writing,*) within three days after the proposed act shall have been reported to them for concurrence; and that, *in failure thereof, such act shall have the operation of law.*" At the last General Convention the following amendment to the whole Article, recognizing, without any reserve or restriction, the rights of the House of Bishops, was *unanimously* adopted: "Article 3. Whenever General Conventions are held, the Bishops of this Church shall form a separate House, with the right to originate and propose Acts for the concurrence of the House of Deputies, and all acts must pass both Houses."

"The progress of this measure," remarks the Hon. Murray Hoffman, (p. 154,) "is a remarkable tribute to the prevalence of just Church views;" and after enumerating various extreme low views which prevailed at different times, he adds,—"When the *absolute veto* was suggested, we find the opposition to it invincible. But the feelings and prepossessions which induced all these actions, (the limitations of the prerogative of the Bishops,) have passed away; and, I presume, it would be difficult to find a churchman in the United States who would now advocate either of them.

Such, then, my friend, has been the striking upward progress in the principles and views of the American Church on the subject of the right of Bishops.

You will at once see that the difficulties which impeded the progress of this measure in the General Convention, would be increased a thousand fold in the Diocesan Conventions. The wrong ground was universally taken at first. The amount of moral courage required in a Bishop to ask for the open recognition of his rights is so great, that we could scarcely expect to find the attempt made. And so we find that, almost without exception, the American Bishops have been "content to enjoy their rights (as they all, I believe, do,) *practically*, while in *theory* they are not recognized."

In the General Convention, it is true, the measure was carried by the Clergy and Laity, and not by the Bishops. But in Diocesan Conventions, individuals of the Clergy and Laity would naturally shrink from bringing forward the measure; some, lest they should be said to be seeking to make favor with the Bishops, while others, more noble minded, would hesitate to do so from higher motives of prudence, as judging that it were better to let the matter alone than attempt to carry it and fail. They would consider it their wisdom to wait the sure growth of a sounder public opinion in the Church on the subject, and meantime set themselves to inform the mind of the Church, through the various channels afforded by the press.

Whatever may be said to this reasoning, the fact is certain, that the growth, in sound Church views, as to the Bishops' right, has been remarkable. The principle was adopted in the Diocese of Vermont, in 1836, and unanimously reaffirmed, after a careful revision, in 1851. In the proposed Constitution of the new Diocese of Minnesota it was inserted, but postponed for further consideration, as it cannot be decided till they have a Bishop of their own. A Canon of the Diocese of Virginia,— *the* "Low Church" Diocese of the American Church,—declaring "that the office of a Bishop differed in no respect from that of other Ministers, except in the powers of ordination and confirmation,—the right of superintending the conduct of the Clergy, and presiding in Ecclesiastical Assemblies,"—retained among her Canons for a series of years, has been repealed. (Hoffman, p. 154.) The most eminent jurists, and best writers of the American Church, agree as to the Bishop's right.* And it is openly and earnestly advocated as the undoubted and inalienable prerogative of the Bishop, by the most influential Reviews, Magazines, and Journals of the American Church Press.†

Such, then, my friend, is the true value of the American precedent; and I leave it to all men of judgment and candour, whether it is more in favour of us or of our adversaries.

Let me, now, briefly sum up for you the results of our re-

---

* Hon. Judge Hoffman. See his *Law of the Church*, pp. 202, 203 & 180, &c. H. D. Evans, LL.D. See three admirable articles by this able and veteran writer, in the "American Church Monthly" for January, February, and March, 1858, especially pp. 12 & 100.

† "American Church Review," "American Church Monthly," "New York Church Journal," "Monitor," of Baltimore, &c.

searches on this most important part of the subject,—the argument from authority and precedent.

In every part of the Universal Christian Church,—except in those parts desolated by the Papal usurpation before the Reformation, and by the Genevan and Puritan discipline since,—and in every Synod of that Church, Diocesan or Provincial, from the day of Pentecost to this day, with the single exception of the Synods of the American Church,—it has always been an unquestioned rule, "that nothing should be done without the consent of the Bishop."

The Synods of the American Church were organized under circumstances peculiarly adverse to all recognition of Episcopal rights; and if the rights of her Bishops were not fully recognized at first, this is only what we might naturally have anticipated.

The whole tone and tenor of Legislation on this subject, in the American Church, has been steadily and uniformly upwards; so that, now, in the General Convention, the Episcopal prerogative has been with unanimous consent established, and, in the Diocesan Synod, is in a fair way of being, with equal unanimity recognized.

And in every single modern Synod in our Colonies, after a careful and sifting examination of the American precedents, the Bishop's right of a concurring voice, in all acts of the Synod, has been reserved.

So that, as regards weight of authority and precedent, we have to choose between these two:—On the one hand you have the laws and practice of the whole Christian Church in every age and country, and of our own modern Anglican Church, in all the Synods of so many separate Dioceses, scattered all over the globe. On the other, you have the single instance of the American Church, whose omissions of this principle, (for so they are, in nearly every instance, and not positive enactments,*) her ablest writers and most influential members, among both Clergy and Laity, deplore, and are earnestly striving gradually to remedy.

---

* Hoffman, p. 206.

Who can hesitate, my friend, to choose between these? I "frankly avow my preference (will the *Association* forgive me for adopting their own eloquent words?) of the well-tried system, which has worked so efficiently" in the Universal Church of Christ from the beginning. "Nor can" I "perceive the wisdom or safety of substituting for the happy example which, in this respect, the rest of the Christian world "presents;" the needless experiments and inventions in ecclesiastical legislation " of the American Church," which she herself is now growing more and more to feel, and confess to be " at variance with the constitutional principles, prevailing precedents, and successful experience, during," now, nearly two thousand years, of all Christian Churches throughout the world.

Several arguments follow this, which I will first carefully enumerate, and then proceed to refute. I gather them to be these:—

1st. That it is inconsistent to desire a Synod at all, and at the same time invest its presiding officer with the power of nullifying its proceedings."

2nd. That, "in the most important act of the Synod, the election of a Bishop, there can be no *veto;*" if, therefore, "the Synod, without a Bishop presiding in it, is competent to sit in judgment upon a matter of the weightiest importance, why must it forfeit, the moment the new Bishop is elected, its competency to legislate in the smallest matters?" "It the Synod be qualified to choose a Bishop for the Diocese, it is contrary to common sense, that on the day of his election he may turn round on his electors and *veto* all their measures, except that of his own elevation."

3rd. That as " the Act of Parliament empowers the Synod, in every Diocese, to 'make regulations for enforcing the discipline of the Church, for the appointment, deposition, deprivation, or removal, of any person bearing office therein, of any order or degree whatever,'—it is " perfectly legitimate to imagine" the Synod proceeding to try and "depose" its Bishops; but this would be perfectly absurd, if the Bishop had a *veto* upon its enactments."

4th. That the Synod would also be "deprived of the right of purging its own floor" of unworthy members, since the Bishop might refuse his assent to such expulsion.

5th. That the Bishop is not "infallible," and, therefore, ought not to be "entrusted with uncontrolled authority."

6th. That "arguments drawn from the analogy of the Queen's and President's *veto* are exploded."

7th. That "the known possession, by the Bishop, of the *veto*, must exert a deadening influence upon the vitality of the Synod in which he presides."

8th. That the Bishop of Quebec possesses already "an immense and varied, in fact, alarming amount of influence,"—which would be "increased and consummated" by recognizing his right to the "veto."

This is a formidable array of objections ; now let us proceed to look carefully into them.

And, first, let me, once for all, expose the groundlessness and fallacy of the assertion which is put forward so confidently, as the foundation of nearly every one of the above arguments, and is carefully and skilfully woven into the whole structure of the pamphlet ; that the Bishop, if his right is secured to him, will have "the power of *nullifying the decisions of the Synod*," and "be invested with *uncontrolled* authority ;" and that the Synod, in that case, would "become little else than an office for enregistering the *acts of the Bishop*."

The first of these assertions is a begging of the question ; for what we claim is this, that nothing is an *act of the Synod* without the Bishop's concurrence.

But, let us grant that the Bishop can nullify the acts of the two other orders, can they not each of them nullify the acts of the Bishop ? Is it reason to say that one party, out of a body of three, can nullify the acts of the other two, when the agreement upon which they deliberate together, is, that nothing shall be deemed an act of the Body, except all three concur in it? The question is thus resolved into this, whether the Bishop should have a voice, as a distinct order, in the Synod, or whether he should have no more influence than any individual Clergyman or delegate?

And the second assertion is contrary to common sense; for, with what show of reason, can the Bishop's power be called *uncontrolled*, when he can *do nothing* without the concurrence of both his Clergy and Laity? If he can do nothing without their united consent, one would think that his power is sufficiently *controlled*. Let this be well considered,—in the Synod, and so far as the powers of the Synod extend, (and they are ample enough,) the Bishop can do nothing without the consent and concurrence of the other two orders. How utterly groundless, then, how surprising is the assertion that, if the Bishop's assent be required, the Synod "become little else than an office for enregistering the acts of the Bishop"! The acts of the Synod can be no more the act of the Bishop, than they are the acts of the Clergy and acts of the Laity; and, with just the same amount of reason and truth, may it be said, that, because nothing can be done in the Synod, without the consent of the Laity, the Synod becomes little else than an office for enregistering the acts of the Laity, and that thus the Laity in the Synod are entrusted with "uncontrolled authority."

In some rare cases, under some supposable, but very unlikely circumstances, the Bishop may find himself unable to agree to something in which a majority of both Clergy and Lay delegates are united; but, whatever the Bishop's own wishes and convictions may be, he can *do nothing, carry nothing, decide nothing, without the consent and concurrence of a majority of both the Clergy and Laity*. All this clamour, then, about "autocratic power" and "uncontrolled authority," is the merest emptiness, and has no foundation of reason or truth. It is well calculated, indeed, to alarm those who will not think; but can have no other weight with sensible, thoughtful men, than to induce pity for those weak enough to employ it.

2. Their next argument is that derived from the election of the Bishop being now vested in the Synod.

Now, in the first place, the *Lay Association* here falls into the fallacy of reasoning, as if the election of a man to the office of a Bishop constituted him a Bishop. This is the doctrine of the Independents, not of the Church of England. A Synod might choose a man to be their Bishop a hundred times over, but he would be no Bishop for all that. It is *consecration* which makes a Bishop, not *election*.

The *Association* speaks of "the now recognized principle of an elective Episcopate." I must confess my inability to understand what meaning this flowing sentence is designed to convey,—for the merest tyro in Church History and Antiquities knows that, however widely, and however long the Church's rights have been usurped in *practice*, the "*principle* of an elective episcopate" has been universally "recognized."

The power of electing, is neither more nor less than that entrusted by the Apostles to the first Christians in Jerusalem, when they said to them, "Look ye out among you, seven men of honest report, full of the Holy Ghost and wisdom, whom *we may appoint over this business.*" (Acts vi., 3.) The brethren *chose* them, but the Apostles *ordained and set them over* the the business. So it is still. A Diocese without a Bishop, is a body without a head. The Diocese, in such condition, is not independent, and at liberty to proceed at once to the election of a new Bishop. No, some larger and fully organized section of the Church takes the widowed Diocese under its care, and is to it a Bishop for the time. And, under its presidency, and according to the laws of the Church, a new Bishop is elected. In our case, the Church entrusts to the Clergy and Laity, under certain conditions, the choice of a head to be set over them. They choose him, and, if he is approved by the Church, he is consecrated, and so constituted their Bishop. The *Lay Association* says, "In the election of a Bishop, there can be no *veto*." This is a mistake. There is always a *veto* upon such election. In the Church they so much (and so justly) admire, no one, no matter how often or unanimously elected, can be consecrated a Bishop, without the consent, both of the House of Bishops and of a majority of the House of Clerical and Lay deputies,—or, during the recess of the General Conventions, without the consent of a majority of the Bishops, and of the standing Committees. So it certainly must, and will be here, when our Provincial Assembly is formed. And even now, all unorganized as we are, there is always a *veto*, at least in the three Bishops called upon to consecrate. The Bishop, once consecrated and set over a Diocese, is invested with "the rule over them"; (Hebrews, 13., 17,) and, however much may be entrusted to the Clergy and Laity, they never go beyond the apostolic precept, which binds them, in all lawful things, to "obey him,"—a precept which, at the least, requires that, in the sacred Synod, "nothing should be done without the Bishop's consent.

3. The next argument of the *Lay Association* is, I confess, astounding. It is this,—that, "as the act empowers the Synod to make regulations for enforcing discipline in the Church, for the appointment, *deposition, deprivation,* or *removal,* of any person bearing office therein, of *whatever order or degree,*" it is "*perfectly legitimate* to imagine *the trial of a Bishop*" by his Synod, and, of course, his deposition; but this (they argue, and it cannot be gainsaid,) would be "perfectly absurd, if the Bishop had a *veto* on all the enactments of the Synod."

This, then, is a specimen of the mode in which the *Lay Association* would have us legislate. They first reduce the Bishop to a cypher in his Synod, by deciding that "the *supreme authority in the Church,* in all matters affecting the Synod," shall be the acts of the Presbyters and Lay delegates, made without, and against the consent of the Bishop; and then, as if this were not enough, they proceed to lay it down, as a perfectly "legitimate" transaction, that his Presbyters and people may proceed to try and depose him! This is pretty well for a beginning. The Clergy and Lay deputies of a Synod to try and depose their own Bishop. This is novel and exciting work; but, gentlemen, is not this going a little too fast? Would it not be well to prepare the minds of the Church for it, by producing a few *precedents*,—with which, of course, you are well furnished, —for so *perfectly legitimate* a proceeding ? But where do you find them ? Not in the American Church, nor yet in the English, nor in any Church whose records are found in History. Not, I fear, in the New Testament; for though SS. Timothy and Titus were empowered to receive accusations against Presbyters, to rebuke and depose them, (1 Tim., v. 1, 19; Titus, iii. 10,) I do not remember that the Presbyters and brethren had power to depose, or rebuke, or even to receive accusations against Timothy or Titus. Nor yet, in the Old Testament, do I remember anything—except the the notable history of Korah, Dathan, and Abiram,—to your purpose ; though this reminds me of the noble Diotrephes, in the New, who so manfully resisted the arbitrary power of St. John. (St. John, iii Epistle, verses 9 & 10.) After all, gentlemen, I am afraid it is not so "perfectly legitimate" a thing as you "imagine." Bishops, yes, even Bishops, dreadful men as they are, little mercy and consideration as they deserve, cannot, I fear, according to the laws of England, any more than they can, according to the Canons of all Christian Churches, be denied the right of being tried, for ecclesiastical offences, by no order or orders of men lower than their Peers.

4. The *Lay Association*, my friend, have a very vivid and vigorous *imagination*. After the brilliant effort we have just been admiring, you will not be surprised at their imagining it by no means an improbable case, that a man so bad as to unite the majority of the Clergy and Laity, in a vote for his expulsion from the Synod, should yet "enjoy a sufficient amount of Episcopal favor and support, to secure for him a *veto* upon the resolution for his expulsion." I can only answer, that, at least in our day, when all things are subjected to the awful tribunal of public opinion, with the whole current of popular feeling setting so decidedly against any exercise of priestly power, such a case is not supposable. A Bishop could never, without the pressure of the sternest necessity, consent to put himself in a position to unite against him, before the eyes of the world, the votes of the body of his Clergy and Laity. His seat, not a bed

of roses at any time, would be made rather too unpleasant by such a course. Besides that, one of the functions of the Synod would be to appoint a proper court to try offenders. It is surely to be presumed, that the Bishop, the Pastor of the whole flock, would be as anxious as any one to preserve the purity of his Diocese, and of its sacred Synod.

5. The *Lay Association* urges, at some length, that the analogy between the right claimed for the Bishop, and the *veto* of the Queen and President, fails, when it is fully and fairly carried out. We may very readily grant that these analogies fail, when pressed in all points. But they only fail, where the head, in either of these two cases, *fails*, and ceases to *be* the *head*, and becomes, for the time, a mere subject or servant. So long as they are, in either case, the *bona fide head* of the State, the analogy holds ; and, in any case, they bear witness to the need of checks and restraints upon the legislation of bodies of men. There is, however, this difference between the Queen and the President on the one hand, and the Bishop on the other. The former derive their authority from the people, (the President immediately, the Queen ultimately,) which may, therefore, be constitutionally restricted, limited, and even ultimately, under conceivable circumstances, lawfully taken away. The Bishop derives his office and authority from Christ, through the Bishops of the Church. The Bishop's authority, therefore, as to its inherent and essential functions, of which the principle at issue is one, as man did not give, so man cannot take away.

6. But they urge again, that "the known possession of a *veto* by the Bishop, must needs exert a *deadening influence* upon the vitality of the Synod, paralyse every manly and independent thought, valuable design, and forcible argument." Why so ? Because, in that case, "the Bishop's projects, the Bishop's wishes, the Bishop's interests, predilections, or even prejudices," must be carried out, notwithstanding the wishes, interests, prejudices, and convictions of the Clergy and Laity ! Here again, appears the palpable fallacy that runs all through the arguments of the *Lay Association* on this question. The Bishop's wishes and projects can no more be carried out, than the wishes and projects of each of the other two orders of the Synod ; they can

only be carried out when they coincide with the wishes and convictions of the rest. The result is not a "deadening influence," but the beauty and strength "of a house at unity with itself."

The *Association* quote and adopt the sentiment of that "grave and experienced English author" they delight to refer to, who says, (p 19,) "It would be quite as well to do without the semblance of legislation, as to be called upon to legislate within the limits which the existence of the *veto* would assign to the Church's representatives." If these words mean anything, they mean this, that the enactments of a Diocesan Synod, in which the Bishop has a voice, would be quite as well dispensed with, and that the only Church legislation worth having, is that which is carried on without, or against the Bishop's consent. Is this the language of genuine, loyal Churchmen,—are these the sentiments of true-hearted members of a Church governed by Bishops?

The best answer to this charge, of a "deadening, paralysing influence," would be furnished by a full history of the acts and proceedings of one Colonial Diocesan Synod, during the last seven years. Let me give you, as a sample of that history, and as illustrations of the "deadening influence exerted on the Clergy and Laity by the the known possession of the *veto* by the Bishop,"—two incidents which occurred at the two meetings of the Synod of Toronto, last year.

The first arose from a motion, "that the Synod do take into consideration the propriety of reviving the Diaconate, as a permanent order, in this Diocese." After (I think) the mover and seconder had spoken, the Bishop rose, and said that he thought it a point not within the province of the Synod, and in which he himself could not act as the law of the Church then stood. Nevertheless, the debate went on; the motion was spoken to, and most earnestly, by a great number of the most eminent clerical and lay members; and the result was, that the Bishop, at the close of the debate, said that "he could not but be deeply impressed by all he had heard; and this much he would say, that if in any parish or mission, the Clergyman and Lay delegates should recommend any person to be ordained a permanent Deacon, he (the Bishop) would take the matter into his most serious consideration." This is authentic, being furnished by a person present on the occasion.

The second incident occurred at Kingston, and the account of it is taken *verbatim* from a letter I received from a friend at the time, "Dr. Bovell's motion on the division of the Services, made a great heat—the Bishop strongly objecting to it—*i. e.*, his power to move in the matter, and referring it to the Provincial Synod. Yet the discussion was ample—not *one* person, lay or clerical, decidedly opposing it, but Mr. ———. Many answered amply—Dr. Bevan, historically and minutely accounting for their amalgamation; [Hon. Mr.] Cameron, showing its unmeaningness; [Rural Dean] Blake, and Hon. Mr. Patton, showing the mischief of it, in wasting the Clergyman's strength, and contracting the field of his labours, to the injury of the destitute population. In fact, every conceivable topic was handled with a skill that surprised me. The Archdeacon of Kingston spoke strongly for the motion. Dr. O'Meara reminded the Bishop that he had his Lordship's permission for such division, as the Litany, &c., were longer in Ojibway than in English, &c."

Now, here is a case in point,—a Diocesan Synod, in which nothing can be carried without the Bishop's consent; the Bishop's "predilections" and views one way, and the *whole discussion* just the other way,—the effect being, at least in one case, that of bringing the Bishop over to the views of the Synod; and yet that Bishop was a man, than whom few have been more reviled as arbitrary and despotic,—the intrepid and self-reliant,—and I will add, as the judgment of that Church he has loved and served so well, and now in his old age, of his once bitter enemies,*—the *great and good* Bishop of Toronto.

Nothing is more unanimously agreed upon by ancient Christian authors, nothing more constantly urged by our modern defenders of Episcopacy, than this, that the Bishop is appointed the head of each Diocese, to be to it *the centre of unity*, just as the father is the centre of unity to his household, and the Pastor to the Parish. The Synod is the Diocese by representation, and

---

* See the great praise given him by William Lyon McKenzie, and *endorsed* by the *Montreal Witness*, 1st January, 1859.

should present a picture to the world, of the unity and love of the Church. How can it be this, except there be agreement? And how *can* there be agreement where the head is set aside, and everything is done without him, or even against his judgment and consent? If "the known possession by the Bishop," of his power, as head and governor of the Diocese, tend to produce unity, quietness, and peace, and love, out of the Synod, why should it not have the same effect within it? Quietness, peace, and love, are better than excitement, bitter debates, heart-burnings, and party strifes. Let us not for a moment think of abandoning that sacred headship which was given to the Church in each Diocese by our Master, to this very end,—"that we all may come, in the unity of the faith, unto a perfect man."

7. But the *Lay Association* once more object, that "the Episcopal chair is already surrounded with an immense and varied if not alarming amount of official, moral, and material influence." "A concentration of power which is unknown to the Hierarchy of the United Church of England and Ireland; is also without precedent in the United States; and which it is believed, finds no parallel in the Church of Rome; and that it is neither necessary nor safe for the Church that this should be increased and consummated by adding to it, besides a presiding influence in the Synod, a *veto* upon all its transactions.

The reference to the Church of Rome, here found, is singularly out of place. The independence of Bishops has never been the policy of Papal Rome. For some ages before the Reformation the Popish Schoolmen and Canonists had been endeavouring to destroy the distinction between the two orders of Bishops and Presbyters. "These," says Dr. Burnet,* "are *the very dregs of Popery*; the Schoolmen raising the Priests for the sake of transubstantiation, and *the Canonists pulling the Bishops lower for the sake of the Pope's supremacy*." In the degradation of Bishops and the usurpation of their rights,

---

* See a full account of this in Burnet's History of Reformation, Vol. I., page 366; and in Bramhall's works. See also Hoffman, p. 210; Pritchard's Life of Hincmar, Bp. of Rheims; and Neander's Church History, Vol. VI.

as in so many other points, Puritanism and Popery are found to be essentially one.

This is a point well worthy of a little further illustration. Burnet says of the Canonists, "That they looked on the declaring Episcopal authority to be of divine right, as a blow that would be fatal to the Court of Rome; and, therefore, they did after this at Trent use all possible endeavours to hinder any such decisions." Let the learned and candid Father Paul* be Burnet's Commentator. He tells us, pp. 603-4, that Pius IV. wrote to his legates at Trent, 1562, "Concerning the articles of the Institution, * * * to make the Institutions of Bishops absolutely *de jure divino*, was a false opinion and erroneous * * And for a resolution he wrote, that either the words *de jure divino* should be omitted, or they should be used in that form which he sent, in which it was said that Christ did institute Bishops to be created by the Pope, who may distribute to them what and how much authority pleaseth it to give them for the benefit of the Church, having absolute power to restrain and amplify that which is given, as it seemeth good unto him." The Lay Association, it would seem, are, with respect to themselves, of the same opinion, and claim the same prerogatives with Pius IV.

The Council of Cardinals at Rome, who prepared every matter for the legates at Trent, wrote to them respecting this point : " That the article of the *Institution* of Bishops seemed difficult and of great consequence, and therefore that they should procure that it should be remitted likewise (*i. e*, to the Pope); which in case they could not do, yet they should *inviolably* observe not to suffer a determination to pass, that it was *de jure divino*." No modern anti-episcopal sect could show a more determined hostility to the divine institution of Bishops, and a more anxious desire to curtail their prerogatives, than has the Papacy ever since the full development of its own policy of self-aggrandisement. Laynez, the General of the Jesuits, admonished the Trentine fathers to "take heed, lest by making the

---

* In his invaluable History of the Council of Trent, translated by Sir N. Brent. Lond., 1670.

institution of Bishops *de jure divino*, they do not take away the hierarchy," *i. e.* the Papacy. And Father Paul in a few words gives us a sufficient impression of how the papal party felt on the whole question. "The legates," he says, "made wonderful factions and interests to quell this opinion." It is well known who among Protestants follow the same course now.

As in the Pilgrim's Progress we find the two giants, Pope and Pagan, arrayed against Christianity, so have they been against Bishops, its chief representatives. Father Paul and Burnet have told us of giant Pope's doings; Jeremy Taylor, in the first sentence of his Treatise on Episcopacy, sums up giant Pagan's : "In all those accursed machinations, which the device and artifice of hell hath invented for the supplanting of the Church, 'inimicus homo,' that old superseminator of heresies and crude mischiefs, hath endeavoured to be curiously *compendious*, and, with Tarquin's device, "putare summa papaverum." And, therefore, in the three ages of martyrs, it was a ruled case in that Burgundian forge, 'qui prior erat dignitate, prior traheb atur ad martyrium.' The priests, but, to be sure the bishops, must pay for all,—' Tolle impios. Polycarpus requiratur.' Away with these peddling persecutions; ἀξίνην πρὸς τὴν ῥίζαν, 'lay the axe at the root of the tree.' Both Pope and Pagan knew 'Ecclesia in episcopo,' that if Bishops are destroyed or degraded so is the Church. This is a point at which the Papist, Pagan, and Puritan embrace.

But to return,—let it be granted, for the sake of argument, that the Bishop *has* all this power, how is this to be increased and consummated by Synodical action ? If *power* were what the Bishops wanted, one would think they would have let Synods alone, for so far as the Synod's province extends they can *do nothing* without the concurrence of the other two orders. To divest themselves of power is certainly a novel way of "increasing and consummating" it ?

The *Lay Association* have given a long catalogue of the prerogatives, powers, and influence of the present Bishop of Quebec. Into questions personal to this venerable Prelate, I must decline to follow the *Lay Association*. This part of their argument, however calculated to excite prejudiced feeling on the great question at issue, is, both in temper and expression, unworthy of Christian gentlemen. It is a pitiful spectacle to see, as we do here and in the *Report* which the *Association* endorses (p. 3), as a faithful " narration of the past," an organized body of Christian laymen thus buffeting the cheek of their own aged and in every sense right reverend Father in GOD. Let us, my friend, turn away and leave them, in this, to the judgment of their own consciences, and,—as our Bishop may well be content to leave his conduct to the verdict of the faithful laity of the Diocese and of posterity.* The legislation of the Synod will be ruled, not by such personal considerations as these, but by the sacred principles of eternal truth, and the unvarying laws of the Universal Church of Christ.

This much however,—passing by all consideration of these sup... sources of influence which are accidental to our present Bishop, and will not belong to his successors in the See,—I may notice that every one of these points will come up, sooner or later, for discussion and legislation in the Synod. And whatever action the Synod takes with respect to the examination of candidates for orders,—the granting or withdrawing of licenses to the Clergy,—with respect to questions of patronage, our dependence upon and connexion with the Propagation Society, which is diminishing every year, and must end,—and the support of the Clergy, will and must be a defining, controlling, regulating, or restricting of that which is now, in the hands of the Bishop, an unlimited and uncontrolled power.

8. One more argument the *Association* throws into a footnote (p. 21). They instance a " notice," given at the last meeting of the Synod of the Diocese of Nova Scotia, " of a motion to abolish the Bishop's *veto*," as a proof that what they are pleased to call "the *experiment* of the *veto* is already furnishing matter for discontent and agitation in the Church."

The true value of this *notice of motion* may be seen in the similar attempt made in the Diocese of Toronto, "to abolish the Bishop's veto," in June last. Persons may give *notices of motion* just as they may " call up spirits from the vasty deep ;"

* See Appendix B.

ut will the motions pass when they do make them? This is quite another matter. It is very easy for persons opposed to this principle, for the sake of keeping alive excitement on the subject, or from whatever motives, to give notices of motions to erase it from the Constitution. Such a notice of motion was given in the Synod of Toronto in 1857, but when it came to the motion itself in 1858 it was negatived without discussion, by probably the most emphatic vote ever given in that Synod. After so severe a rebuke, such *notice of motion* will not be given in *that* Diocese again for a long time to come.

If the history of the Synod of Nova Scotia were known this ' notice of motion" would produce no surprise. A certain number of the Clergy with their flocks have refused from the first to join the Synod at all, and used all their influence against the so-called *veto*. But it was carried, and (I am assured by those who know,) will still be maintained by the almost unanimous voice of the Synod. The loud talk of the *Church Witness*, and the *notice of motion*, may sound important to us at a distance, but they attract no attention and produce no effect in the Synod of that prosperous Diocese.

In another foot-note (p. 22) they quote the Lord Bishop of Huron, as saying, that "he thought that, after two years deliberation, he would be acting against every right, were he not to accede to the repeated request of the majority of the Synod." I am afraid this authority will not help the *Lay Association*. If the Lord Bishop of Huron thought such a power, so vested in the Bishop,—as the *Lay Association* does,—"unscriptural," "dangerous to the Bishop, and to the independence of the Church," certain to "exert a deadening influence upon the vitality of the Synod, and a power "which makes the attempt to legislate a farce, and discussion worse than useless,"—surely he would have said, that "if this rule were established, it would be against his will, and he would never use it."

But, with all due deference, I am sure that, in some cases, his Lordship would not think and do as he is reported to have said. If the Clergy and Lay delegates were to seek to enact something which the Bishop in his conscience thought to be wrong, or, in his judgment, clearly and seriously injurious to the Church, and, refusing his consent to it, they were to unite in proposing it again; would he, in that case, "accede to their request?" Impossible! No conscientious good man could do so. But such cases,—cases which, in the nature of things, can occur but seldom,—being excepted, what his Lordship said, is no more than what was said by the truly venerable, and as truly venerated Bishop of Toronto, in his short but memorable speech, on the motion to repeal this very rule, in his Synod, last year; and what would be said by every Bishop, under the same circumstances? "Is it to be supposed that I would set myself against the united wishes of the Clergy and Laity of my Synod?"

I have now finished my review of this pamphlet of the *Lay Association*. I have gone carefully, and, I think I may say, *patiently*, through their arguments against the two great principles at issue, and examined those principles. Whether that examination has resulted in a complete and satisfactory refutation of the objections alleged, you must judge. One thing I think I have sufficiently proved; *that the Lay Association are not worthy of the confidence of the Church.*

They claim to be the assertors of the rights and liberties of the Laity. They prove their claim by a most determined effort to cut off the great body of the Laity from all possibility of exercising those liberties and rights.

They claim to be the impartial instructors of their brethren in the country, and to give them reliable "information," such as may help them to form their "principles and opinions," on points of the last and most sacred moment. They prove their claim by suppressing facts within their knowledge, and which had a direct and all-important bearing on the subject in hand, denying others of equal weight,—it is to be hoped, through ignorance,—and colouring, or unfairly stating, those they do bring forward.

Their mode of dealing with plain facts, while professing to give information, needs explanation. One of two things must be true. They are either very dishonest men, or very ill-informed. In either case, they are not worthy of the confidence of the Church.

I have shown that the course they would have us take, with

reference to the right of the Bishop to a distinct and concurrent voice in the decisions of the Synod, is, under the whole circumstances of the case, without a single precedent in the history of the Christian Church ; and that it is, on the contrary, in direct violation of her laws, and opposition to her universal practice.

I have examined the precedents of the American Church, and have shown that, so far as they bear upon our case, they are entirely on our side.

All their objections to the rule reserving to the Bishop his right, have been seen to rest upon the supposition,—put forward again and again to endless forms,—that the Bishop would thus have absolute and uncontrolled power. I have shown that this is a gross and transparent fallacy ; and that, with this right secured to him, the Bishop's power is so thoroughly controlled and limited, that he can do nothing,—so far as the Synodical action extends,—without the consent and concurrence of each of the other two orders.

And I have, I think, made it clear, that to give up this principle, is, in so far, to abandon Episcopacy, and to pull down the Bishops, the *overseers* of the Church, from those thrones of rule and judgement on which the Holy Ghost has set them.

Seeing, then, that the *Lay Association* and their principles are so little to be relied upon ; and that, in favour of the principles we advocate, we have reason, scripture, and so great a right of authority as the laws and practice of the Universal Church, let us, my friend, let all loyal Churchmen, unite together in an immoveable resolution to establish those principles in the constitution of our Synod.

The *Lay Association*, finally, append a draft of a constitution, which " proposes to *endow* the Episcopate with a certain reserving power." This, no doubt, is very generous of the *Association*. But I, for one, as a true member of the Church of England, and the Catholic Church of Christ, am as strongly opposed to *endowing* the Bishops of the Church with powers not entrusted to them by its Founder, as I am to taking away those sacred rights He committed to their charge. I will be no party to the introduction of changes into the constitution or system of the Church. Such as we have received her, let us transmit her, unchanged,—with her brightness undimmed, her glory unsullied, her bulwarks of strenghth and defence unshaken,—to our children. If Christian Bishops never have had such a power as we claim, they ought not to have it now. But if, in all time hitherto, the rights for which we contend have been held by Christian Bishops, let us beware how we rashly stretch forth our hands to pull them down from the seats of rule on which Christ has set them. In God's holy name, let us, through evil report and good report, rally round them, and maintain them in their place.

That the Laity will be found, as they ever have been, loyal to the Church of their Lord, and maintainers of its sacred principle, I am deeply convinced. I have no fears for them. The true people of the Church have always been conservative of her rights, and are so still. They will come to see that this is a question between responsible and irresponsible headship; and that when the Bishops and Clergy are put under the feet of the *people*,—the truth is, that Bishop, Clergy, and people, are put under the feet of two or three Laymen of wealth, influence, and ambition. The Bishop is responsible for the care of the Church; of this responsibility he cannot divest himself. Those who are ambitiously snatching at those rights, are not, and never can be responsible,—they cannot clothe themselves with responsibilities not entrusted to them. When once they thoroughly understand this, it will be easy for the people to choose between them. Perhaps they will remember some of those so-called Pilgrim Fathers, who fled from England to escape from what they had been persuaded to believe was Episcopal tyranny, "found the little finger of my Lords Brethren," Lay and Clerical, thicker than the loins of "my Lords Bishops."

No, my friend, our people may not all thoroughly understand this question, but they are not yet prepared to degrade their Bishops into the mere underlings and officials of a committee of influential Presbyters and Laymen. Their Christian instincts, their own natural good sense, would revolt from so unnatural a proposal. History, my friend, has not been written for nothing, and that history bears witness that Christian Bishops, when free and independent, have ever been the true, as they are the natural guardians, the defenders unto death, of the liberties and rights of the Christian people; and that when the Pope would lord it over God's heritage, he had first to deny the divine authority, and inalienable functions of all other Christian Bishops, and to destroy their independence. And history bears witness to another fact—that the faithful Laity never deserted a Christian Bishop who stood up manfully in defence of any part of the Church's holy system, her Evangelical truth, or Apostolical order. Who stood by the great Ambrose, when, in defiance of the Roman Emperor's mandate, and at the peril of his life, he held his Church closed against the Arians, and by their zeal and determination terrified the tyrant into giving up his impious project? The faithful Laity of Milan. Who stood by Athanasius, when, in defence of the Catholic faith, he stood against the world, and ever refused, in all his exile, to admit over them any other Bishop? The faithful Laity of Alexandria. Who stood by the seven Bishops, when they boldly opposed King James, in his attempts to bring Popery back again upon the ruins of the liberties of his country, and by their hearty open support, made the heart of the unhappy King and his minions to quail? The faithful Laity of London. And the faithful Laity of old Quebec, believe me, my friend, will be no whit behind them; and our beloved Bishop, when he sits at the head of his Synod, will find that a disloyal false-hearted faction is one thing, and the faithful Laity of the Diocese another; and that when this important principle is brought before them, with one voice they will answer and say, LET NOTHING BE DONE WITHOUT THE BISHOP.

Farewell, my brother, and join with me, at this time of trial, in the saintly Bishop Wilson's petition, in days far worse than these,—a petition which shows how well he knew wherein consisted, under God, the strength and safety of the Church :—

"Grant that all Bishops and Pastors may be careful to observe the sacred rights committed to their trust :—

"That Godly discipline may be restored and countenanced :—

"That such as are in authority may govern with truth and justice; and that those whose duty it is to obey, may do it for conscience sake :—

"That Christian people may unite and love, as becomes the disciples of Jesus Christ."

APPENDIX A.

" The small and *unprogressive* Diocese of Vermont," say the *Lay Association,* insinuating that the Diocese is " unprogressive," *because* its Bishop has his prerogative secured to him in the Convention. Perhaps some of my readers may be familiar with the learned works of the " English author of grave character and great experience," and may remember what he says on this point; (Letters of Anglicanus, &c., p. 18,) that "a glance at the growth of the Diocese may suggest the thought, that the existance of a Bishop's *veto* may paralyze the energy of a Church, and make a Diocese very quiet, but very stationary."

The accomplished and excellent Bishop of Vermont answered one *English Author* sufficiently at the time. On that answer I cannot now lay my hand. The following extracts from a letter lately received from a Clergyman of high standing, connected with that Diocese, will be a sufficient answer to these ungenerous assaults :—

" The Diocese of Vermont, within the four or five years following the adoption of that Constitution, nearly *doubled* its number of Clergy and Parishes. Then, owing to the Bishop's losses, and the overthrow of the Institutions at Burlington, together with the constant and severe drain from emigration to the Far West, the Diocese hardly held its own, though with a slight gain in the numbers of its communicants. Latterly it has taken a fresh start, and is now in so vigorous a condition, that, poor as it is, it subscribed, and has paid over $20,000, to establish a Theological Seminary of its own (besides what the Bishop has raised elsewhere); and the number of its communicants has increased 10 per cent. *since last June.* There has not been the slightest connection between that article in the Constitution, and the depressed state of the Diocese during a few years.

" *All* our soundest and best writers agree in regard to the Bishop's right. And what is more, even those Low-Church Dioceses, where they would vote down the proposition as High-Church, do really act on it with extra.ordinary vigor. In Ohio, for instance, on the question of dividing the Diocese, the motion was laid on the table, on the express ground that the Bishop's approval had not been privately *asked in advance*, which is going a great deal further than any High-Churchman demands. That a Bishop should exercise a *veto*, after hearing the full discussion on both sides, and knowing the voto of both Clergy and Laity, is a very different thing from *privately* yielding to his whims, without any argument or public application of his sense of official responsibility. It is like getting a judge to decide a case in his parlor, on *ex parte* application, without open trial and the hearing of Counsel."

APPENDIX B.

The slanders circulated, through the press and otherwise, against the Bishop and Clergy of Quebec, are endless. I will select one instance as a specimen of the reckless way in which charges of the most damaging character are brought by the men of this party, in the public newspapers, against the Bishop, whom, when it serves their purpose, they profess to venerate.

The *Quebec Gazette*, the chosen organ of the *Lay Association*, undertook (11th Oct., 1858) to review the Bishop's Pastoral, of the 31st August. In that review the Bishop is charged with several "glaring errors of fact." One of these "glaring errrors of fact" is this. The Editor of the *Gazette* says :—

" We have only time to point to another glaring error of fact in the pamphlet in question. (The Bishop's Pastoral.) It was stated that it was only after a meeting had been held in the Court House, and a petition got up against any change in the original act, that a counter-petition was forwarded. Now, it is also a notorious fact, that the counter-petition in question, was published in a morning contemporary several days before the other numerously and influentially signed petition was thought of or written."

Now, here is what the Bishop actually stated (Letter, p. 11) :—

" It was in consequence of the *announcement* of this meeting, and of the petition with which it was connected, that the counter-petition was prepared and forwarded."

The Bishop says, "it was in consequence of the *announcement* of the meeting, and of the petition," that the petition in favor of the Bill was prepared. The *Gazette* quoted him as saying, "it was *only after the meeting had been held* in the Court House, *and a petition got up* against any change in the act," that this was done. Thus the Editor of the *Gazette* makes the Bishop say the direct opposite of what he did say, and that too, with the Bishop's words before him in print!

And what are the facts of the case?

The meeting in question was first *announced* in the *Gazette* of Friday evening, the 23rd of July, and advertized in the *Mercury* of the 24th. The *Gazette* of the 23rd adds, that one of the objects of the meeting was "to remonstrate against any changes in the law, and if necessary *by Counsel* at the bar of the House." Was not this an *announcement* of an intention to *petition?* How could the meeting "remonstrate against a change in the law," except by *petition?* How could Counsel be heard at the bar of the House, against a Bill, except in support of a *petition?* So, I suppose, every one would understand it. The "announcement," then, "of the meeting, and of the petition," was made on Friday, the 23rd July, and "the counter-petition" was, in consequence, drawn up, signed, and forwarded, on Monday, the 26th. Where, then, is the Bishop's "glaring error of fact"?

Again, the *Gazette* says :—

" It is a notorious fact, that the counter-petition in question was published in a morning contemporary several days before the other petition was ever thought of or written."

But what, again, are the facts?

The meeting and petition against the Bill, were *announced* on the 23rd July. The meeting was held on the 26th. That meeting (See Appendix to Address of Lay Association, p. 8, ii. Resolution.) appointed a Committee, "with authority *to petition the Legislature.*" The "counter-petition" was not published in the *Chronicle* until Thursday, the 29th. That is to say, the petition in favor of the Bill was not published until three days after the Court House meeting had appointed a Committee, with authority to petition against the Bill. And yet the *Gazette* says, "It is a *notorious fact,* that the counter-petition was *published several days* before the other petition was ever *thought of!*"

Now, *who is guilty of "a glaring error of fact?"*

It is a serious matter to bring so grave a charge as this against one whose character for truth and honesty is so precious to the Church as is that of her Bishop's. And the above single specimen of the accuracy of this party, in stating facts which were lying in print before them, should surely be sufficient to convince all reasonable men of the necessity of receiving their statements with some degree of caution.

Lovell & Gibson, Printers, Yonge Street, Toronto.

ERRATA.

The reader is requested to correct the following errors with his pen before perusing the Pamphlet.

Page 12, line 20, after *minority*, insert (").

" 14, " 10, for *facts* read *feats*.

" 19, " 5 from bottom, after *than* insert *that*.

" 33, " 10, for *the right* read *this prerogative*.

" " " 14, for *Synow* read *Synods*.

" 35, " 7, for *increasing* read *unceasing*.

" " " 21, for 1857 read 1787.

" 36, " 2, for *half* read *back* and erase the comma.

" 36, " 19, for *and* read *of*.

" 38, " 20, after *them* insert (").

" 40, " 20, for *Synod* read *Synods*.

" 42, " 14, for *in fact* read *if not*.

" 43, " 17, for *become* read *becomes*.

" 45, " 13, after *never* insert *can*.

" " " 17, after *consent* insert (").

" 48, " 19, for *one Colonial Diocesan Synod* **read** *our Colonial Diocesan Synods*.

" 50, " 23, after *transactions* insert (").

" 52, " 22, after *tree* insert (").

" 52, " 4 from bottom, after *and* insert *sources of*.

" 52, " 6 from bottom, after *it* erase (?).

" 53, " 4, for *narration* read *narrative*.

" 54, " 9 from bottom, after Synod insert (").

" 56, " 11, for *to* read *in*.

" 56, " 15, erase *the*.

" 57, " 2, for *strenghth* read *strength*.

" " " 14 from bottom, after *remember* insert *how*.

" 59, " 2, of 2nd paragraph, for *one* read *our*.

" 62, " 5 from bottom, for *Bishop's* read *Bishops*.